A HUSBAND FOR ADELINE

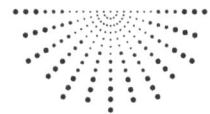

CYNTHIA WOOLF

FIREHOUSE PUBLISHING

Copyright © 2020 by Cynthia Woolf

All Rights Reserved. No part of this book may be reproduced or transmitted in any form or by any means, electrical, digital or mechanical including but not limited to photocopying, recording, scanning or by any type of data storage and retrieval system without express, written permission from the author.

Published by Firehouse Publishing
Woolf, Cynthia

Cover design copyright © 2020 Lori Jackson Design

CHAPTER ONE

June 02, 1871

Adeline Brady stood on the landing outside the room in this saloon she shared with her father overlooking the boisterous gaming down below. The poker room held ten tables for poker or Faro but also had two roulette wheels, one on each end of the room. Every table was full, even the roulette. Dolly Matthews, the owner, would make a killing tonight, just like every night.

Saloon girls with painted faces and short, low cut dresses, wandered around the room, some serving drinks. From her high perch, she watched her father play cards. He required her to watch just in case he needed her.

She was tired of being the pawn in her father's games. Her father was a gambler. When Alastair Brady was up and rolling in the chips, he was the greatest dad around. But when he was losing, he did things…terrible things…like wager her virginity in the game.

So she signed up to be a mail-order bride. Her fiancé, Josiah Colter wrote her several letters and he'd finally sent the money for her travel expenses to the mail-order bride service she used in New York. Now she had to go to New York and meet with the woman who owned Brides for the West.

She thought about the trip she'd make to get to Central City in the Colorado Territory. When she left Virginia City, she hadn't needed Josiah's money for the ticket. She had squirreled away almost five-hundred dollars over the last thirteen years. Every time Alastair gave her money after he won, she bought some little things so he'd think she'd spent it. That way when he ran out of money and came to her for some, she could honestly say she'd spent the money on the items she bought. And she always bought things that would need replacing, like face cream and her lilac and rose waters.

She supposed she could take her money and move away somewhere to start a new life, but she had few skills except poker. She knew how to play that game very well. Her mother taught her to bake and cook. Those were the skills she wanted to use. She wanted to be a wife and have a home. A real home…and family. A husband and children of her own. Becoming a mail-order bride would give her that.

Not one to trust her fellow man, for the trip to New York, she placed twenty dollars in coin and small bills in her reticule and the rest in the belt around her waist, under her clothes.

Sneaking out in the middle of the night, while Alastair was still playing was the only way she could leave. She always went to their rooms about eleven o'clock each night so she could sleep before he came in, sometimes not until morning.

If her father found out what she was up to, he'd lock her away until he needed her again. She couldn't wait for the stagecoach where her father might see her and stop her from leaving. Earlier in the week, she'd arranged to rent a horse from the stables. The stable master had a horse waiting for her.

The man held the horse for her while she tied her carpetbag to the back of the saddle and then mounted. He looked up at her. "When you get to Carson City, if Toby isn't in the stable waiting, go to the house behind the stables and knock on the door."

"Thank you, Mr. Herbert. I appreciate your help." She galloped toward Carson City, sixteen miles away.

The trip took her almost two hours even though she galloped as much as she possibly could without hurting the animal.

When she reached Carson City she turned the horse into the stables. Toby was waiting for her and was awake even though it was about two in the morning. The owners of the two stables were brothers and liked to have the opportunity to rent the steeds again and again. That arrangement was perfect for her purposes.

Once she boarded the train she finally released the tension and her body relaxed. The farther away from Virginia City she got the better she felt.

She slept for a while that seemed like days but was in actuality only hours. The first major stop would be in Chicago. On the way there, she went through some of the most beautiful country she'd ever seen. The Rocky Mountains left her breathless. Covered in pine trees they looked purple from a distance.

Once out of the mountains, she traveled through prairie and high desert. She saw hundreds maybe thousands of buffalo. The animals were huge and some grazed so close to the train she could tell they were covered in brown hair and seemed to have curly cottony looking hair covering their shoulders.

She saw more rabbits than she'd ever seen in her

life and light brown antelope jumped and frolicked around the buffalo.

When the train reached Cheyenne she would change trains and board one to Chicago and then she wouldn't change again until she reached New York. The entire trip from Carson City to New York City took about three weeks by train.

Three weeks later, she arrived in New York and took a Hansom Cab to Brides for the West, mail-order bride agency. Addie paid the driver and stood on the curb for a minute looking up at the brown brick building. Brownstones they called them. They were three stories high with two windows facing the street on each level. Each building was attached to one just like it on either side.

She knocked once and entered. A pretty blonde woman in her early forties was filing papers in one of several document filing boxes behind a magnificent dark wood desk. She looked over at Addie.

"Come in, my dear, come in. I'm Emily Johnson. What can I do for you?"

"Hello, I'm Adeline Brady." Addie walked forward and held out her hand.

The woman set down the files on the top of the desk, reached across and shook Addie's hand.

"Miss Brady. I'm so happy you were able to make the trip. I realize this is an inconvenience for you but I like to get to know my ladies before I send them to their new husbands."

"Completely understandable. It also will give me time to do a little shopping while I'm here for a new coat and boots for winter in the Colorado Territory."

"Very good. Let me take you next door and you can meet the other ladies."

Addie met the three ladies who were living in Emily's boarding house at the moment. Cordelia Jameson, Marilyn Gentry, and Diana Roberts. The ladies, especially Cordelia became friends in the short time she was there. She thought she might have saved Cordelia when a man assaulted her in the house, knocking her to the floor. Addie thought he might have hurt her more if Addie hadn't come into the room.

She was only in New York for a little more than three weeks before she was back on a train to Denver. From Denver she took a stagecoach to Golden City.

Miss Johnson wired to Josiah just before Addie left New York and told him when to meet her. The train could be delayed and she knew he might not meet her. If so, she would get a room, have a bath, and then wait outside each day until he arrived.

Luckily the train arrived on the day it was

supposed to, though she did wish she could have a bath before meeting her intended.

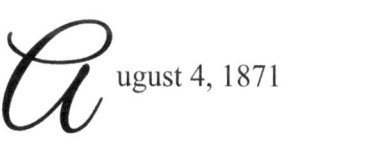

August 4, 1871

In Golden City,, the stagecoach driver helped her down from the vehicle. As with all the stagecoaches she'd ridden the little stairs were treacherous especially for a woman with heels on her shoes or in her case button boots. They were the best shoes she had for traveling.

She stood on the porch of the Golden City Hotel, her two carpetbags beside her, and waited for Josiah. Her pulse raced as she realized she'd be meeting the man she'd spend the rest of her life with. Addie looked at the hotel somewhat wistfully, still wishing she had that bath she wanted so much.

From out of the hotel a tall man approached her. She couldn't see much of his face. His Stetson was pulled low and he kept his head down but his dark brown hair was just a little too long and curled over his collar.

"Miss Brady?"

"Yes. Are you Mr. Colter?"

He removed his hat and looked down at her with the deepest blue eyes she'd ever seen and shook his head. "I'm afraid I have some bad news. Josiah was killed in a cave-in of our mine, three weeks ago." He paused. "Along with my wife." He held out his hand. "I'm Douglas Latimer."

Her stomach dropped to her toes. Dead. Josiah was dead. What would she do now? Where would she go? How could she have children and the family she wanted so much? Adeline shook his hand and tried to keep her voice from shaking. "Your wife?"

His lips formed a straight line. "I have no idea what she was doing there."

She realized that her loss wasn't as great as this man's. He'd lost two people that were probably the closest to him. "I'm so sorry. You must be devastated losing your wife and your friend at the same time."

He ran a hand behind his neck. "I admit it has been difficult. Would you like to go inside and refresh yourself? We could have something to eat and finish this discussion."

"Yes, I'd like that very much."

He spread his arm wide. "After you."

She bent to pick up her bags.

"I'll get those." He picked up her bags with his left hand and put his right on the small of her back, guiding her into the hotel.

She looked behind her toward her back and then

back up. The gesture seemed a little forward for someone she'd just met. Maybe that's the way they did it here.

"Where can I freshen up?"

"I have a room here. I need to check on my daughter anyway. I left her sleeping to come get you."

Her eyes widened. "You left her alone?"

"I didn't have much choice and I made sure she was safe. Follow me, please."

Adeline followed him. He could be trying to take advantage of her, but she'd been in enough saloons and dealt with enough men doing just that. She wasn't worried between the knife in her boot and the small, custom Colt strapped to her leg, she could handle herself.

Mr. Latimer directed her to the first door down the hall from the lobby. Not the room she was expecting because if he tried anything everyone would hear her scream. Of course, being able to hear what was happening in the room may have been his reason for getting the room to begin with. As they approached, she heard a cry come from inside.

Mr. Latimer passed her, put the key into the lock and rushed in as soon as the door opened. He dropped her carpetbags by the door propping it open.

He went to the bed, which had a drawer sitting in the middle of it, picked up an infant and cuddled it to his chest. "Oh, oh, yes, you woke up alone and I'm so sorry." He patted the baby on the back. "Yes, I'm so sorry." Mr. Latimer turned. "This is my daughter, Emilia. I call her Emmy. She's two months old."

The baby was so small. She hadn't seen one that small in years. She'd made friends with a woman in Virginia City named Angel. She had a son about the same age or at least the same size. So tiny and so helpless.

Angel needed help in order to go back to work as a saloon girl.

She asked Addie to watch him while she worked. Addie agreed immediately. She loved babies and little Eric was no exception. He was the one person she missed the most when leaving Virginia City but Angel said she was leaving, too.

"I'm leaving in the morning. I've made a match through a mail-order bride service and the man is willing to accept me and Eric.

And yet, Douglas took care of Emmy and quite competently.

Seeing him with his daughter and how gentle he was with her, Addie had no qualms about being alone with him. She moved her bags and closed the door with a click. The room was nicely appointed with a double bed, dresser, small table and chairs under the window.

He turned his deep blue eyes on his daughter. "Miss Brady, I have a proposition for you."

She clasped her hands in front of her to stop their shaking. "What kind of proposition and does it concern Emmy?"

Mr. Latimer nodded. "Yes, I want to marry you. I need a mother for my daughter. The marriage would be one of convenience only. I don't expect to have relations with you. I won't fall in love with you and I warn you against falling in love with me. You would sleep with me as we only have two bedrooms. Emmy's crib is in the second bedroom."

His proposition was the answer to her problems. She'd been about to marry a man she'd never met, why shouldn't she marry a man she had? "Yes."

"I'm gone a lot so you'd have the…" He swung his head toward her.

"Did you say yes?"

Now, her stomach did somersaults. "I did. When can we get it done?"

He tilted his head and furrowed his brows. "Why would you do this? You don't even know me."

Addie gazed at Emmy. She was a beautiful child with blonde hair. She wondered if the infant took after her mother. "I know you love your daughter enough to offer marriage to a stranger. Just so we can be clear, I don't believe in divorce, so if you can live with that, then we have a bargain and your daughter will have a mother and you'll have someone to help you raise her."

He smiled. "I don't believe in divorce either. After we've come to know one another perhaps we'll want to take our marriage to the next level. I would like more children, Miss Brady, at sometime down the road. I don't want Emmy to be an only child. I was, and I don't recommend it."

Addie dropped her gaze, his eyes seeming to see right through her bravado. "I was as well and I agree. I do want to have more children, but we can discuss that as our marriage progresses. May I hold her?"

"Of course." He handed his daughter to her.

Addie gazed down at the infant. She was light as a feather and Addie was almost afraid she'd break her, but she needed to get used to holding a baby again. She would now be responsible for her. "Oh, yes. There you go, sweet girl. We'll get to know each other very well."

Emmy sniffled and gazed at Addie with her daddy's deep blue eyes. "Oh, poor sweet baby, you're just soaked. Shall we get you into some dry clothes?" Addie looked up at Douglas. "Do you have clean diapers and clothes for her?"

"Yes, of course." He walked over to one of the chairs under the window and opened a saddlebag from which he pulled two flannel diapers a small wool soaker, socks, and a long gown. "Here you go. I'll get you a washcloth to clean her first."

"Thank you."

He nodded and went to the dresser where a pitcher and basin sat, returning with a damp washcloth.

Addie made quick work of cleaning and changing Emmy. She hadn't done it since baby Eric in Virginia City.

Douglas took the wet clothes and laid them over the footboard to dry.

When Emmy was clean and dry, she picked her up and cuddled her. "There you are sweet thing. All clean and dry. Now I bet you're hungry, too." She turned to Douglas. "Mr. Latimer, what do you feed her? Milk?"

"Formula from a bottle." From the other side of the saddle bags he got a bottle with powder on the bottom. "Just need some water." He poured water from the pitcher into the bottle and shook it for a minute or two. "Here you go." He handed her the filled bottle. "She'll only drink about half of it before she goes back to sleep and I think you should call me Douglas. Mr. Latimer seems a bit formal for the man you'll be marrying in an hour or so."

"An hour. I'll finish feeding her and then wash my face and hands. I want to change into something clean. You'll have to turn your back."

Douglas lifted his eyebrows. "You're not making me leave the room?"

Addie wasn't sure she should tell him the truth, but what choice did she have? He should know up front what her background was. "I'm only a little more modest than a man, Mr., er, Douglas." Her heart pounded and her hands shook. She put a hand on her hip. "I was raised in saloons by a father who liked to bet my virginity to cover his hand at the poker table. I hate gambling and I hope that's not something you indulge in very often."

She cast her gaze down, remembering her life since she was ten. "Luckily for me, he always won those hands and I never had to *pay up*." Addie looked back up at him. "You seeing me in my corset and bloomers will not embarrass me. If my background bothers you, you should let me know now so I know what kind of clothes I need to put on." *What if he says he doesn't want to marry me now? What if he doesn't want a bad influence around his daughter? Will I really have to go to a saloon and play cards? I would hate that.* Though she hadn't prayed since her mother died, she prayed now. *God, please don't let him reject me.*

Now, she might have to use the money around her waist to live on and to stake her in a poker game. *Do they allow women to play poker in Golden City?*

He was quiet for a moment. "Would I have to worry about you being around my daughter? Are you the bad influence you seem to want me to think you are?"

"I'm not. I will never set foot in another saloon if you marry me. I won't put your reputation at risk."

His gaze never left her. "Is there a difference in the clothing you'd wear if you have to work in a saloon?"

"Yes. If I have to go make a living at a poker table in a saloon, I'll wear very different clothes than if I become your wife."

He looked at his daughter. "I would like you to become my wife, Miss Brady."

Relief surged through her and she could breathe again. "Call me Addie, please."

Emmy was asleep in her arms but Addie knew she had to be burped. "I'll burp her and then change her."

"I can take care of her." He put a towel on his shoulder and reached for his daughter.

Addie passed the baby to him.

He turned his back and faced the window.

Addie stood at the foot of the bed with one of her carpetbags on the bed as she removed the top dress from the bag. "Thank you. I'll get ready." She washed her face, neck and hands, then stripped down to her corset and bloomers before donning a nice, but plain, blue calico dress. It buttoned up to her neck and made her eyes seem even bluer. The style was simple with blouson sleeves and relaxed skirts that weren't made for lots of petticoats.

"All right, you can look now and thank you for being a gentleman."

Douglas had a towel on his shoulder for Emmy's spit up when he burped her.

Addie watched him and fell a little in love with him. He was so good with his tiny daughter. *I can't do this. He warned me not to fall in love with him and yet I find myself doing just that. I must stop. I'm simply setting myself up for heartache.*

He held Emmy with one hand under her head and the other under her bottom. "You did so good my sweet girl. Yes, so good. Are you full now? Ready to go marry your new mama?"

Emmy smiled.

Addie knew the baby couldn't understand the words yet, but she understood her father's voice and the pleasure in it.

Douglas gazed over at Addie. "You look quite pretty in your dress. Shall we go? We can get dinner in the hotel restaurant afterward and then come back here. That will be about her bedtime. We'll stay here and leave tomorrow morning. It's much too late to leave Golden City now."

She wasn't used to getting compliments and her face heated. "That's fine. I'd rather travel in the daylight anyway. I'd like dinner. I have to admit I'm hungry."

He lifted his brows. "It's nearly five-thirty. Would you rather eat first?"

Addie shook her head. She wanted this over with before he changed his mind. "I'd rather get married first, if you don't mind."

Douglas's smile reached his eyes and showed his straight, white teeth.

"I don't mind at all. Shall we go? I've got the preacher on notice."

"You seem awfully sure of yourself. What if I'd said no?"

"Then I would have to find someone else, probably one of the saloon girls who have been after me to marry them."

That's why my background doesn't bother him. He was prepared to marry a saloon girl, if necessary. Her back straightened. She'd known many saloon girls over the years and ninety-nine percent of them were very caring women. "They're probably very nice women. Just because they work in a saloon doesn't mean they aren't good women. I've had many that I would consider friends. They were definitely good women in a bad circumstance."

"I know. But since I've met you, I'd rather marry you."

Addie's cheeks warmed at the compliment.

They walked down the boardwalk to the church. People passed them and some of them greeted

Douglas. Apparently he was well known and she would guess since they all seemed to be smiling, that he was well-liked, too.

The church was a white clapboard building. Only the small steeple with a bell and a cross on top marked the white clapboard building as a church.

She hadn't visited one for many years. Entering the building, she found the vestibule cool and inviting.

Douglas continued into the sanctuary.

The reverend was waiting for them. "Douglas, my son. I'm glad you made it so quickly. I have another marriage to perform after this one."

"Well, Reverend Black, let's get this ceremony out of the way."

The tall, thin man wearing a black suit and stiff white collar, waved his hand for them to approach. "Of course. Come forward and stand in front of me. Young woman you stand on Douglas's left."

She walked up the center aisle, carrying Emmy, to where the reverend stood.

He took a small pad and pencil from his pocket. "What is your full name, miss?"

She smiled at the man of God. "Adeline Louise Brady."

Reverend Black wrote on the pad. "Very good and Douglas what is your full name?"

"Douglas John Latimer." He looked down at her.

She was glad she was holding Emmy or everyone would see her hands shaking.

The reverend added that information to the piece of paper. He smiled at them. "Very good. All right here we go. Dearly beloved we are gathered here in the presence of God and these witnesses."

What witnesses? Addie glanced around and noticed a young man and woman had joined them, the woman at her side and the man at Douglas's.

The woman gazed at Emmy. "Can I hold your baby?"

"No, but thank you," said Addie.

"Now," continued the reverend. "Do you Douglas John Latimer take this woman, Adeline Louise Brady, to be your wedded wife? To have and to hold, through sickness and health, for richer and for poorer, and promise to keep yourself only unto her for as long as you both shall live?"

"I do." His deep voice was loud and clear.

"Repeat after me. With this ring, I thee wed."

Douglas nodded. "With this ring, I thee wed." He took a plain gold band from his pocket and placed it on her finger.

It was just a little tight but she preferred it that way.

Addie smiled and looked down at her hand.

Reverend Black turned toward her. "Do you, Adeline Louise Brady, take this man, Douglas John

Latimer, as your lawful wedded husband? To have and to hold, through sickness and health, for richer or poorer, to honor and obey, and to keep yourself only unto him for as long as you both shall live?"

"I do." Addie was glad her voice was steady, clear and didn't betray her nervousness. "I don't have a ring yet, Reverend."

The reverend smiled. "That's all right. By the grace of the Lord, God Almighty, the town of Golden City and the Territory of Colorado, I now pronounce you man and wife. You may kiss your bride."

Addie looked forward to being kissed. It would be the first time.

Douglas gave her a quick peck on the lips and reached up with his left hand and rubbed his thumb along her lips. "I'll give you a real kiss after we put Emmy to bed," he whispered.

She was married—for better or worse. She'd do her best to make this marriage of convenience work. But Addie wanted more children and knew there was only one way to get them. She'd have to seduce her husband.

CHAPTER TWO

*A*rriving back to the hotel, they stopped at the front desk and got her a key to the room. Douglas walked to their room first.

"I want to check Emmy." His eyes twinkled when he looked at her.

Just what was behind the twinkle. What motivated her new husband? She'd find out more over their meal.

"Would you hold her while I get her clothes and a clean diaper out?"

"Of course. She's my baby daughter now, too. What are you doing with the dirty diapers?"

"I have a burlap bag that I lined with oil-cloth that I'm putting them in."

She smiled down at the baby in her arms. "That's

a good idea. You're my daughter now, too, aren't you, Emmy?" Then she kissed the baby's cheeks and her little button nose. She smoothed her hand over the baby's blonde hair and thought she'd put a ribbon in it tomorrow for the trip home…wherever home was.

Douglas watched her with a smile on his face. "You're already falling in love with her, aren't you?"

"What would make you say that?" She waved a hand in front of her. "It doesn't matter, you're right. How can anyone not love such a sweet baby? I do already love her and no one will take her away from me. Not even you, should you for some reason decide you don't want to be married to me anymore—"

He held up a hand. "That won't happen. Ever. As I told you, I don't believe in divorce."

"Good. Let's go eat before my growling stomach scares Emmy."

Douglas laughed. "All right let's get you fed."

Addie smiled. Everything would be all right and yet there was a niggling bit of doubt. How could she be so lucky?

Addie looked around at the restaurant. Wallpaper with pink roses covered the walls. A dozen or more tables graced the room each with a crisp white tablecloth. In the middle of the tables were pint-sized canning jars filled with wildflowers.

Two windows on the left side of the dining room were covered with lace curtains, the weave tight enough to give privacy to the people sitting there and yet allowing lots of light in.

Four chandeliers hung from the tall ceiling shedding light on the tables below. The effect was quite charming.

A pretty, redheaded waitress seated them. She wore a lovely white blouse with mutton sleeves and a simple black bombazine skirt. An apron was tied at her waist. She pulled a ticket book from the pocket in the front of the apron.

The woman tickled Emmy under her chin. "Oh, isn't she just the sweetest little thing and she looks just like you, Mama."

Douglas covered his mouth.

Addie heard his chuckle. She glared at him and then looked up at the waitress. "Like me?"

"Of course, with your blonde hair and blue eyes, she's just your image."

"Thank you. That is so nice of you to say."

"Now, what can I get you folks to eat?" She gestured to a sign with the day's selections on it. "The special today is beef stew with sourdough bread and apple pie for dessert."

Addie's mouth watered. "That sounds wonderful. I'll take the special please."

The waitress lowered her ticket book. "It is. We have probably the best chef in town and she loves to make stews because they take so many different ingredients. She makes her beef stew with carrots, onions, potatoes and turnips for a little bite. It's quite tasty, if I do say so myself."

Douglas gazed up at the red-haired waitress. "Make that two of the special. You've convinced me it's the best choice."

The woman smiled. "If you don't like it then dinner is on me."

"Oh no." Douglas held up a hand. "I couldn't do that even if I hated it. Besides now I'm sure it's the best on the menu."

"You won't regret it. My name is Betty. If you need anything just let me know."

"We will, Betty. Thank you," said Douglas.

Betty turned and headed toward the kitchen.

He returned his attention to his new bride. "Do people always call you Adeline? I'd like to call you Addie if it wouldn't upset you."

She grinned. "Addie is fine. It's what my mother called me when I was young. My father never called me anything but Adeline. He said it made me sound more valuable."

"Your father sounds like a royal—"

She put a finger over her lips. "Shhh. He was. Is. Believe me. Where do you live? Josiah mentioned a mine. That would be somewhere in the mountains to the west of here would it not?"

"He was correct. Our mine, The Old Glory, is in Central City which is about twenty miles from here give or take a mile. Though you can't actually see the mine, you can see where it is from my home…our home. We need to leave early tomorrow morning. I have a large buggy. It's lighter than a wagon but it will still take us around three to four hours to get home. It's mostly uphill and I don't like to push the horses more than necessary."

"That's fine. I'm normally an early riser."

"I am, too. Even more so since Emmy was born."

Addie chuckled. "Yes, I understand infants need to be fed several times during the night. I kept my friend's baby while she worked. I'm quite familiar with how infants are, at least how Eric was. He had to be fed and changed three times each night, so I'll be able to help you now. We can take turns."

"I'd hoped that would be the case."

"I want you to know that you can count on me to be there for Emmy."

Betty returned, putting a large bowl of stew in front of Addie and one in front of Douglas. Then she set half a loaf of sourdough in front of them with a crock of butter and a bread knife.

Addie held Emmy in her left arm and picked up her spoon with the other. "The stew smells heavenly."

He nodded. "It does. Would you like a slice of bread?"

"I'd like the heel if you don't mind."

"You may have the heel. I would have taken it if you didn't. I know it's not the favorite piece for most people."

She sighed. "When you have a loaf, fresh from the oven, that first slice, that heel, with butter on it…" She closed her eyes, remembering when her mother would bake and give her the heel with it practically floating with butter.

"Do you bake?"

Addie opened her eyes and saw amusement on Douglas's face. Her face heated as she realized she'd almost made a spectacle of herself. "Sorry. I was remembering my mother again. And yes, I do bake. I haven't had a place to do it since my mother died thirteen years ago. Then my father decided to play poker for a living. I look forward to having a kitchen to cook in. I like to cook and bake. I hate keeping house, but I'll do the best I can."

Douglas cut off the heel of bread, buttered it and handed it to her. "I'm sure you'll do fine. You have to do a better job than I did. I'm afraid the house is a bit of a mess."

Addie took a bite of the stew. "Betty was right. The stew is excellent." She waved him off and then blotted her mouth with her napkin. "As to the housework, I'm hoping it's not anything I can't handle… and if it is, I'll let you know you need to hire a housekeeper, if possible."

Douglas dipped his bread into the stew bowl. "Fair enough. I will probably be at the mine most days after you're settled in. We are still clearing it. We got to the bodies easy enough. They were close to the entrance like they were fleeing from something." He took a bite of the bread. "You're right the stew is excellent, as is the bread."

Addie smiled. "Sourdough is my favorite, as long as it's not too sour. This is perfect. Betty wasn't kidding when she said they have a wonderful cook." She took another bite of the stew. This time getting a turnip. "Mmm."

"What?"

"It's just the meal is so good."

He swallowed. "That it is."

"Who is the *we* you're referring to? I know you and Josiah had the mine. Do you also have men working for you?"

"I have about one hundred men working for me." He continued with his dinner.

"My goodness, your operation is much larger than Josiah let on. As to why Josiah and your wife were close to the front, maybe they heard the mine start to collapse." *Josiah and Douglas own a mine and have many people working for them. Douglas is much more stable and probably much richer than I thought. I won't have to worry where my next meal is coming from or being bet in a poker game.*

"Or they heard or saw the person who set the blast."

Addie's eyes widened. "You mean they were…" She looked around to make sure they weren't being overheard, but no diners were at the tables near to them. Still she whispered. "Murdered?"

He nodded with a frown. "I believe so but I can't prove it yet. I will and then I'll go to the authorities. If they won't do anything then I'll take care of it myself."

Addie looked around at the other diners and then leaned forward, careful of Emmy, still whispering. "You wouldn't do anything that would get you in trouble would you? You have two people counting on you now. I can't take care of Emmy properly if I have to find a job because you got yourself killed or thrown in jail."

Douglas grinned, put an elbow on the table and set his chin in his hand. "Miss me already, huh?"

Addie rolled her eyes. "Not even. But since it

appears we've finished our meal perhaps we should go back to the room. What time do you put her to bed?"

"Usually around seven o'clock, so by the time we get her ready for bed, she may want to eat."

"I can feed her and get her ready for bed."

"Good idea." He waved Betty over.

The pretty redhead returned to the table. "What can I get for you all?"

"Nothing, just the check."

She put a hand on a hip. "But you haven't had your pie yet."

Douglas looked up at her with those big blue eyes of his. "Is there any way we can take them with us? We're in room one right off the lobby."

She smiled. "Sure. I'll bring them out on a tray with forks. Would you like a milk or coffee to go with them?"

Addie grinned. "Oh yes, I'd love a glass of milk."

Douglas lifted his chin. "Make that two."

Betty wrote on her ticket book. "Okay. I'll bring them to you if you want to go on down to your room."

Addie put a hand on her arm. "That's so kind of you, Betty. Thank you very much."

Betty waved her off. "Ah shucks. Ain't nothing. Now, you get on to your room and I'll be there in a few minutes."

Douglas took Emmy from Addie and headed out

of the dining room and across the lobby. When they reached the room, he was holding a sleeping Emmy.

Addie took the key from him and unlocked the door, letting him in first and then closing it after her.

Douglas laid Emmy on the bed.

She started to cry.

"She's soaked again. It's a good thing I brought lots of clothes for her."

"I noticed all the clothes drying when I was in the room before." Lying on the headboard, the backs of the two chairs and the footboard of the bed were clothes and diapers, hung to dry.

"If you want I'll change her," said Addie.

"Thank you, that would be much appreciated. I'll gather the dry garments."

Addie suspected they would reuse the diapers and clothes for the trip home. Although she didn't know how many clothes and diapers he still had in those saddlebags.

When they got home the first thing she would do is boil water and wash Emmy's dirty clothes. She knew many people just dried the wet diaper and used it again, but Addie didn't hold with that practice. Traveling was a special situation and she understood having to reuse the clothes and diapers but she believed clean diapers and clothing was the best way to keep the baby rash free.

Douglas handed her a diaper from the saddle bags.

"I have one more diaper after this one." Then he gave her a clean nightshirt. "But I did buy more thick flannel from the Golden City Mercantile. We can cut that with my knife if we need to. I had thought to wash the material first but," he shrugged. "We do what we have to do."

Addie had already stripped Emmy and cleaned her with a washcloth. She took the clothes from him, diapered and dressed the baby.

Emmy began to fuss and then let out a high pitched squeal.

Addie picked her up and cuddled her. "Oh, sweetheart, are you hungry? Your daddy has a bottle ready for you. Don't you, Daddy?"

"Yes, ma'am, I do." He handed Addie the bottle.

She sat on the bed and fed Emmy. The baby sucked happily. About halfway through the bottle, Emmy started falling asleep. When the baby was fully sleeping, Addie took away the bottle and burped her. Then Addie put her in the drawer Douglas had prepared for her to sleep in.

"She's so beautiful. Emmy is a good baby, you know."

"I think so but then I'm not an impartial judge."

"I'm not anymore, but from the beginning, she's been quiet and happy unless she's wet or hungry. You can't ask for more than that from a two-month-old baby."

"No, I suppose not."

Addie sat on one of the chairs at the table under the single window. "Does anyone ever call you Doug or always Douglas?"

He moved the saddlebags to the floor and sat in the other chair. Then he leaned back, crossing his left leg over his right knee. "One of my teachers called me Doug."

"How old are you? I'm twenty-three."

Douglas ran a hand through his hair. "I'm thirty-one and before you ask, I was married for seven years. Elizabeth had several miscarriages before we had Emmy and she was a difficult birth." He uncrossed his legs, leaned forward, resting his arms on his knees and then leaned forward, hanging his hands in between them. "I remember we fought that night. I don't even remember over what, and she burst into tears before running out of the house." He looked ups at Addie. "I couldn't leave Emmy alone so I stayed, expecting her home. She never came and then I learned about the cave-in. I got the neighbor, Edna Smith, to watch Emmy while I went to the mine. The miners had already pulled the bodies out when I got there. I was shocked to see her body along with Josiah's."

"I'm so very sorry for your losses. But since you'd had a fight maybe she went to talk to him. A shoulder to cry on so to speak."

A knock sounded at the door.

Douglas held up a finger. "I'll be right back." He walked to the door and opened it.

Betty stood on the other side carrying a tray with two pieces of apple pie and two large glasses of milk.

Addie rushed to the door and took the tray. "Thank you, Betty. Your kindness is much appreciated."

Douglas pressed a five-dollar gold piece in her hand. "Thank you for everything."

Betty put the gold piece in the pocket of her skirt and waved a hand in front of her. "Ah, it 'tweren't nothin'."

Douglas returned to the table.

Addie set out the pie and milk with a fork and napkin.

He sat and picked up his fork. Before continuing with their conversation, he took a bite of the pie. "Wow, this is good."

She swallowed. "It really is. I hope when I get to baking I can do as well. Now, you were saying about Josiah and Elizabeth?"

"Yes, I don't think she would have gone to him. She and Josiah didn't appear to be friends. It seemed to be all they could do to remain civil to each other when he came for dinner."

Playing devil's advocate, Addie said what she thought they both were thinking. "Perhaps they were better friends than you thought and their relationship was an act so you wouldn't suspect anything."

Douglas frowned. "I've thought of that, but I just can't make myself believe it." He stood and lit both the lamps in the room, as it was starting to get dark.

"I don't have any other ideas, I'm sorry."

"Don't be sorry. It's not your fault. Are you finished with your pie?"

"Yes, couldn't eat another bite."

He pointed at her plate, "Mind if I do?"

"Not at all." She pushed her plate with its bite or two of pie on it across the table to him.

Addie finished her milk while he ate.

When he was finished, he stacked the plates in the center of the table.

"You're very neat."

"Not really. Just trying to impress so you won't run screaming when you see the house."

She laughed. "Now you are scaring me."

"I suppose we should get to bed. Morning will come early."

"Yes, it will." Addie stood and went to one of her carpetbags. She dug around inside and found her nightgown. She'd bought a new one before leaving New York City. The one she had was ratty-looking from five or six years of wear. "Will you close your eyes again or should I just turn my back to you?"

"I'll close my eyes."

Addie smiled. She figured he would sneak a peek. He was a red-blooded American male after all. She made quick work of putting on the nightgown. "I'm done. You can open your eyes now."

His eyes popped open. "You look lovely."

"Thank you." She reached up, pulled the pins from her hair and put them on the bureau. Then she found her brush and gave her waist-length hair one hundred strokes until it shone in the lamplight. She climbed into the bed on the side nearest the wall. "Your turn now."

"You have beautiful hair. It's almost the same color as Emmy's. No wonder Betty thought she was your daughter. Guess I'd better change now." He reached up and started with the buttons on his shirt.

Addie closed her eyes after he took it off. She'd seen her father without his shirt and she caught a cowboy changing his shirt in the back of the saloon but she'd never seen one that looked like Douglas. His arms and shoulders were taut with muscles that moved when he did. He had a flat stomach and narrow waist.

She felt the bed go down on his side as he slipped under the blankets. "Goodnight, Douglas." She blew out the lamp on her nightstand.

"Goodnight Addie. Sleep well." He blew out the lamp on his side.

The room was thrown into darkness. The only light was from the moon outside.

"You, too."

Addie awoke wrapped in Douglas's arms with her legs thrown over his. She felt her face heat and her stomach turn over. She'd never been so embarrassed in her life, but to her dismay, she liked the way it felt to be in his arms. Nevertheless she held still and tried to think how to get out of this without waking him.

"I see you're awake."

The deep timbre of his voice rolled over her like silk.

"I am, and I'm so sorry. I must have gravitated to your warmth."

"Understood." He unwrapped his arms from around her.

She lifted her leg and rolled to her side of the bed.

"I'll get dressed and then go for coffee if you'd check on Emmy. I think she's awake but she hasn't been making any noise like she wanted to get up, just little gurgles."

He got out of bed.

Addie also rose and, keeping her back to Douglas, went to Emmy in her makeshift crib on the floor at the foot of the bed. "Good morning, baby girl. How is my sweet girl this morning?"

Emmy waved her arms and pumped her legs.

Addie picked her up and kissed her lips. "Shall we get you a bottle?"

Douglas dressed while she had her back to him and now wore his pants and shirt.

He held out his arms for the baby. "I'll hold her while you dress and then I'll make her a bottle before I go."

"Thank you. I won't be but a minute." Addie wore the same dress as yesterday. It wasn't dirty and she didn't see any point in putting it back in the carpetbags just to get another one out. She only had three dresses and would rotate them as necessary. "I'm done. I'll take her and change her clothes. Do you have another baby gown in your magic saddle bag?"

He laughed. "As a matter of fact…" Douglas produced a fresh, white baby dress outfit. "These are the last two I brought with me. One gown and one diaper. I'd like to get home before she wets these completely."

"Do you have more diapers at home that have been washed?"

He shook his head. "No, but do have that material to make them. Thick, soft flannel. The thickest they had."

"Good. I'll cut them out when we reach your home."

He handed Emmy to Addie. "I'll make that bottle and then get coffee for us."

While Addie cleaned Emmy and changed her into fresh clothes, she watched Douglas. He loved the baby more than anything, which showed on his face.

"I'll be right back."

He walked out the door.

Addie watched him go. Maybe it was too soon, but she wondered if, eventually, he would love her a little, too, regardless of what he said now.

CHAPTER THREE

The trip to Central City went faster than what she expected. The beginning of August and the weather was hot. She unbuttoned the neck of her dress to get some air on her heated skin and unwrapped Emmy from the blanket so she wouldn't get too hot either.

"So tell me about yourself Addie. I knew Josiah was getting a mail-order bride but I never thought it would be someone as beautiful as you."

"Thank you. I've told you the most important things, except maybe that my mother died when I was ten. Up until then I lived in a real house and not in a room above a saloon."

"You said your father used to bet your virginity in games of chance."

"He did. Which was another reason why I went to

New York first. He never would have thought I would go so far away."

"But now you're back in the West. Do you expect your father to find you?"

"I'm hoping not, but with Central City being a gold mining town, he could very well come here. That circumstance would not surprise me. But the fact that I'm married will stop any of his shenanigans."

"You hope so anyway."

That was true. She did hope so. There were so many things that could go wrong if her father showed up.

"Let's not think about that now. Just the thought of it turns my stomach." She waved her hand around them taking in all the scenery. "But these mountains are beautiful. I came through them on the train, but getting to see them up close…well, it's amazing. Some of them have snow on top. Did it already snow here?"

He shook his head. "No, not down here anyway. The tops of the mountain peaks can get snow at any time during the year, even in summer."

He slapped the reins on the horses' rears.

They drove through a little town. She wondered if he lived outside the town since he didn't stop anywhere.

"Is this Central City?" This town looked like any other mining town she'd been in. Lots of saloons and one church. She knew which was most popular with the miners.

"No. We have another mile and a half to go. This is Blackhawk, another mining town."

They drove on and approached the town she would live in. Just like the town of Blackhawk, Addie saw at least a dozen saloons first and foremost. Farther into town she saw a mercantile, butcher, baker and sundry shop and another handful of saloons, a general store, and a hardware store.

"Why have a mercantile *and* a general store? Aren't they the same thing? They are elsewhere."

He nodded. "And they are here, too. The couple involved divorced and the husband opened the general store since the wife kept the mercantile. Her family gave them the money to open the establishment in the first place."

"Do you prefer to shop at one place over the other?"

He shrugged. "I usually go to the general store because it is owned by the man, but you can patronize whichever store you desire."

As she gazed at him she lifted her chin and tilted her head a bit. "That's good, because I will probably patronize the mercantile, but I also plan on seeing which store has the best prices. I don't care about their fight or their divorce, I care about saving money."

Douglas laughed. "Looks like I married the right wife. I'm into saving money, too." His smile faded. "But not at the expense of my men. I would never build a mine shaft that was not shored up so it wouldn't collapse. Never. That's another reason I believe Josiah and Elizabeth were murdered."

"Does that mean Emmy and I are in danger? Should I be extra cautious? I have a knife in my boot and I keep a gun strapped to my leg. I never knew when I'd need them, especially in a mining town."

"I noticed both of those when you undressed last night."

She cocked an eyebrow and dipped her chin as she looked at him. "You weren't supposed to be looking."

He lifted one shoulder. "What can I say? I'm a man and I want to see my wife naked. Although all I saw was your back. Lovely back, by the way."

She chuckled. "I've been around men all my life. I figured you'd look which is why I turned my back on you."

"Touché."

He took a road which went above the town and pulled next to a house, which was quite small. It appeared to be the perfect size for a little family…like theirs. Next to the house was a large barn.

"I'll carry your bags if you'll take Emmy."

"Of course. It would be my pleasure." She

rewrapped the baby in the blanket so she wasn't too squirmy.

Douglas came around and helped her down.

"Is there a key?"

"Yes. Which reminds me. Keep the door locked at all times. Sometimes drunk or desperate miners come up here from the saloons looking for anything they can exchange for another drink or hand of cards."

She nodded. "I'll remember that." Addie carried Emmy to the front door and waited for Douglas to unlock it.

He went in first.

She followed while he held open the door.

"Emmy's bedroom is down the hall, first door on the right. Ours is the next door."

She felt her face heat to points on her cheeks. Turning away, she walked to Emmy's room and found the white walls decorated with pink unicorns underneath a blue sky with clouds floating in it. "This is lovely. Did your wife do this?" A small bed was against one wall, Emmy's crib forming an "L" with that bed. There was also a small bureau with a basin and pitcher and a Tallboy dresser. At the end of the crib were pails for the wet and dirty diapers.

He nodded. "Elizabeth always fancied herself an artist."

"Well, I'd say from the detail she put into the unicorns, she definitely was."

"Thank you. That comment would have pleased her very much."

Addie smiled, not sure what she should say to that. She laid Emmy in the crib and unwrapped her from the blankets, which, of course, she had wet. "I assume you didn't leave any clothes for her here, so I'll just change her diaper and leave her in the crib until I can get more clothes washed and dried. Will you put on some water so I can do her laundry? I'll cut a diaper out of the flannel you bought if you'll get me a pair of scissors."

"Okay. I'll be right back. I'll bring in the flannel and the groceries before I start the water, so you can at least diaper her."

"Thank you. I'll leave her on the blanket until then."

Douglas set down Addie's carpetbags and left. He returned quickly and handed her the thick, soft flannel and a pair of shears, before leaving again.

She cut the fabric so it made several large diapers. Then folded one of them so it was small enough for Emmy now. This made the diaper very thick. She rubbed the diaper pin in her hair to put oil on it and make it easier to go through the cloth. The pin was almost too small to go through all the layers, but with these she probably didn't need the wool soaker, but she'd put one on Emmy anyway.

She left Emmy playing with a baby rattle and

went to wash the bottles and find another one she could prepare for the baby when she was ready to eat.

Entering the kitchen she found Douglas lighting the stove. One of the buckets sat atop it.

"Do you have any clean bottles for Emmy?"

"In the cupboard to the left of the sink."

She gazed around the room. A stove was on the wall to her right and the back door to her left. Next to the door she entered through, stood a table and eight chairs. Looking at the table, she decided he was definitely planning on a large family. Along the wall across from the table were cabinets and drawers, a sink with a pump on it and an icebox. "Your kitchen is very nice. I've never been in a kitchen with a pump on the side of the sink. In New York they had running water and in Virginia City and other towns like that, the pump was outside and served many families."

"That used to be the way this was, but Elizabeth wanted water in the house, so we put in the pump and tied it to the well outside. There is still a working pump outside if you should ever need it. The Smiths next door use it for their water, and I use it to water the animals. We have a cow and chickens in the barn in addition to the horses."

She stared at him. "What do you expect me to do with them? I can look for eggs, I guess, but I don't know how to milk a cow."

He shrugged with a small upturn of his lips. "I'll teach you."

She put her hands on her hips. "So what are you doing while I'm taking care of your daughter, cooking, washing laundry and cleaning the house?"

"I'll chop wood for the fireplace and the stove."

Addie crossed her arms over her chest. "And?"

Douglas ran a hand through his hair. "I guess I could milk the cow."

"Good. Then I'll gather the eggs. I don't believe we should both be out of the house at the same time."

Douglas put the second bucket on the stove. "I hate to leave Emmy alone. She usually plays in her crib for a while in the mornings." He grinned, the movement reaching his eyes and they crinkled at the sides. "That usually consists of her sucking on her hands. She hasn't figured out yet about the thumb and how good it is to suck on it. Emmy is a really easy baby. Unless she's very uncomfortable like she's messed her diaper then she lets you know and wants to be changed right now."

"What about since you've been gone? Don't cows have to be milked every day?"

"They do and I've had the boy next door doing it in exchange for the milk and any eggs he can find. His dad is one of my miners but he likes to gamble, so there are times there is little food in the house." Douglas frowned. "I've tried talking to the man, but he can't or won't help himself. So I started giving them half my milk and eggs. They needed them more than I do. If you need me to change that, I can. They knew I'd be marrying Josiah's bride if she'd have me."

Like any woman in their right mind would turn you down especially after they met Emmy. And I'm definitely in my right mind.

She took his saddlebags, which he'd thoughtfully, brought in and left in the kitchen, and took all of Emmy's clothes and diapers out of them. "I'm sure I can make do. How many chickens do you have?"

"Two dozen. And most of them are laying hens."

"So you get two dozen eggs every what? Week?" She looked under the sink and found a basin which she pumped water into. Then she put the messy diapers in the basin, and rinsed them out, readying them to be washed.

"No every day."

Addie laughed. "We won't need that many eggs every day by any means unless you sell them to the general store or the mercantile." *He's very generous. I know people that would only sell them regardless of the needs of the family next door. I like that.*

"I used to. Until I found out they didn't have food next door."

"We won't need more than about six or eight eggs every day, and that's assuming I bake…a lot."

"If you like to bake, we could share those with the family next door as well."

Addie snapped her fingers. "I think that's a wonderful idea, husband. When I bake a cake or cookies, I'll make a double batch. How many are there in the family?"

He stopped and looked at the ceiling like he was counting people in his head. "Seven. Eight if you include the father and he brings a lunch to work every day. Where they find the food for that, I have no idea."

"We'll do the best we can to help them. Maybe the father will come to his senses, but that has not been my experience with men like him. The only thing that matters to men like that is the next game, the next bet and the next drink."

Douglas sighed. "I'm afraid you're right. Joe Smith will never change and Edna will just end up with another baby. Did I tell you she's expecting? That will make seven children ages ten and under." He put up his hand and counted down on his fingers. "There's Joey, Claire, Larry, Rami, Sarah and Audrey who is the youngest at just eleven months old."

She furrowed her brows and narrowed her eyes. "That's appalling. How can a man do that and then leave them without food? I've a good mind to tell him what I think of him and the way he treats his family."

He shook his head before moving to the counters

and leaned against them with his hands on either side of his hips. "Edna would not thank you for that. She doesn't like to take charity but she does because of her children, but if you anger her husband, she might not get what she does now."

Addie released a deep breath. "I suppose you're right. I should keep my opinions to myself and just do what I can for the family. What if I bake them a cake and Joe eats it without leaving them any? I know his type."

Douglas paced. "Then only bake them cookies. They can eat some of those before he comes home to get his lunch and go to work. He rarely comes home for a meal which is probably why he doesn't care." He lifted his shoulders. "As long as he has food, why should he care?"

Addie walked over and placed a hand on his arm. "Douglas. You're getting worked up over something you can't change. I suppose you could always dock his wages for food for his family, but how many of your other workers would you have to do that for? How many do you not know about?"

He blew out a breath and then sighed. "You're right. We can help this family. If I find out about any more, I'll help them, too."

"I'm not saying we shouldn't help, but aren't there any churches in this town? Churches are known for their charity work. Perhaps we could give donations for food for the poor."

"I don't know. The "men of God" are not so much here. Gold does strange things to a person, even preachers and priests. I've seen plenty of them at the tables in the saloon before I had Emmy. I'm not proud of it, but I used to play poker myself, sometimes. Probably more than Elizabeth wanted me to."

"I hope you've gotten that out of your system, because I won't put up with it. What am I to do if you start abandoning me and Emmy? Find a man who'll cherish us the way we deserve?"

His eyes narrowed with his rising anger but then just as quickly his mouth turned down as he blew out a breath.

He looked her in the eyes. "I don't like the thought, but yes, you should do exactly that. Emmy is the most important person in my life and if I'm not caring for her, for you, then you should find someone who will. But I swear that will never happen."

Addie smiled. "I don't believe it will, either. I just want you to know where I stand."

"I do." He grinned. "I've said those two words more in the last couple of days than in the last year."

Addie laughed. "I'll remember that and try to get you to say them more often. On our anniversary if nothing else."

Emmy began to fuss. Her little cries carried to the kitchen.

Addie turned in the direction of Emmy's room.

Douglas dropped his hands to his pants and wiped them off. "I'll get her."

Addie shook her head. "Bring her diaper with you if it's wet."

He brought the baby into the kitchen. "I think she was just lonely and didn't want to be ignored."

"Ah, poor, sweet thing. She was right. We were ignoring her." Addie noticed steam coming off the buckets. "Looks like the water might be ready for the laundry tubs. Do you have them?"

Nodding, he handed Emmy to Addie. "Hold her and I'll bring them in."

"Oh, I love holding you." She talked to the baby, rubbing her hand over her little back. "I think we should always make your diapers larger and then fold them so they are thicker. You're still dry." After Douglas left the room, she pondered a question to her daughter. "I wonder if your daddy would really let us go if he did start behaving badly? I wonder?"

CHAPTER FOUR

While Addie did laundry, Douglas watched Emmy and fed her. When she was through with Emmy's clothes she went into the bedroom, pulled off her undergarments and her dress. She donned a clean dress, chemise and bloomers, eschewing her corset. Her skin was raw on her sides and under her breasts, where it had rubbed during her long trip from New York to Central City. She added her traveling clothes to the pile and picked them all up.

As she passed Douglas in the living room rocking Emmy in front of the fireplace, she gazed down at them and smiled. "Um, if you have clothes that need washing, give them to me now."

"I do. Will you hold Emmy? I usually put her in her crib when I do this and when I did the chores. It's a little chilly in here at this altitude even at the end of August. I need to build a fire. Then I'll give you my clothes."

"All right. I'll take these clothes into the kitchen and then be back." She took her laundry into the kitchen and then returned. "Okay, give me our precious girl."

He placed Emmy into her arms and then bent in front of the fireplace.

In no time, he had a blaze going and the living room was no longer chilled at all. Just the opposite. Addie went into the kitchen which was also too warm and so she walked back to the living room and sat as far away from the fireplace as possible…on the green striped sofa under the window which had matching solid green curtains which were currently closed. The effect was not what she would have chosen, but was not unpleasant. She opened the curtains and let sunlight into the room.

Douglas returned with his arms full of clothes.

"I take it you haven't done your laundry in a while?"

He had the good grace to grin and look sheepish.

"I was having the Chinese laundry doing my clothes, but with all this murder and brides and marriage on my mind, it's been a while. Do you mind? I can still take them to the Chinese laundry if you do."

She pursed her lips. "I don't want anyone thinking I'm too lazy to do my husband's washing. Put them on top of mine in the kitchen. Do you have a basket I can carry the clean clothes to the clothesline to dry?"

"Sure I'll bring that in, too, and make sure the clothesline is up properly. The clothespins are in a cloth bag tied to the basket."

Addie spent the next two hours doing their laundry. She probably should have scrubbed them harder but she thought unless the clothes were very soiled the action of scrubbing them only wore them out sooner.

By the time she finished, it was nearly one in the afternoon. She was exhausted and still needed to make something for lunch. But when she went inside, she found Douglas had prepared a meal.

"Ah, right on time. Lunch is served. Sorry I don't have any bread and I don't know how to make biscuits, so we have just the scrambled eggs and ham. Oh, and milk. Joey left a quart jar in the icebox."

Addie couldn't have been happier. She went over to Douglas and gave him a big kiss on the lips. "Thank you. I was preparing to come in and figure out what to make for lunch. Where's Emmy?"

"In her crib, sleeping…I hope."

"We really should get groceries. Next time we go to the general store, I'll go with my note pad and prices. And then I'll do the same at the mercantile."

"Wow. I'll have to remember to cook more often if those kisses are my reward, but I will have to show you how a husband and wife kiss."

She lifted her brows. "There's more than one way to kiss?"

Douglas smiled. "Oh, my dear wife, many more and one that is my favorite way. Would you care to know?" He patted his lap.

Addie cocked her head. "I would be interested to learn." She walked over and settled herself on his lap, her back stiff.

He was tall, warm and smelled wonderful. Sandalwood. Her favorite man's scent. It was the only thing about her father that she always liked. She was fairly short at only five feet four inches, so sitting on his lap made him only slightly taller rather than a lot.

Douglas angled his head, slanting his lips over hers.

Her eyes drifted closed.

He kissed her gently, and then pressed his tongue along the seam of her lips.

Addie's eyes flew open and she gasped.

He pressed his tongue in her mouth.

She tasted his coffee, from just before she came inside and him. Addie relaxed and closed her eyes, enjoying the kiss. Her heart beat fast and she was afraid he could feel it pound with her pushed up against his chest.

Finally, he pulled back, placing little kisses on the corners of her mouth.

"Well, what do you think?"

She kept her gaze down. "I like that very much. Is that the one you like, too?" she whispered.

He grinned at her. "Yes, my dear. That is my favorite."

"I think it's my favorite, too. Can we do that again?" She wrapped her arms around his neck.

Douglas didn't answer with words. He took her lips in a kiss.

This one was even better than the one before.

He pulled back. "You'll be the death of me if you learn everything as fast as you learned how to kiss."

"I like learning new things."

"When you're ready, I have some other things to show you that a husband and wife do together."

She lowered her gaze and her cheeks heated. "When I'm ready? To make love you mean."

He nodded. "When you're ready to try to have children or even before, I've many things to show you."

She gazed up at him. "You do? Are they like this kissing? Because I like this."

He grinned. "Even better." He took her lips again with his.

Emmy cried out.

Addie broke away from Douglas. "Our daughter

awakens. I'll get her. I've cut the rest of the flannel into large diapers. They do last her much longer."

Douglas released her and she scooted off his lap.

"Be right back." She pointed at the stove. "Eat while the food is still warm."

Addie walked into Emmy's room. The baby was crying hard.

"Oh, hush now. You're fine. I've got you." She picked up the wet baby and cuddled her. "Did you think you'd been abandoned, hmm? I will never leave you, sweet girl. Never, for as long as I draw a breath. Let's get you changed. How does that sound?"

Emmy sniffled and laid her head on Addie's chest.

When Addie started to lay her back in the crib, she cried.

"I'm not leaving. No, I'm not leaving." She quickly cleaned and changed her diaper. Emmy had to go without a dress or nightgown because all of those were outside drying. Addie placed the dirty diaper in a bucket with a round piece of wood over it to keep down the smell. "All right. You're all clean and dry. Time to go and see Daddy." She wrapped the baby in a blanket to keep her warm.

Douglas followed Addie's instructions and ate while she was gone. By the time she returned he was ready to take Emmy from her and let Addie eat her lunch.

"After I finish eating I need to make a list for the

general store. We have to have more than eggs and ham in the house. I'd like to go to the butcher, too. When do you get ice next for the icebox?"

He pulled on his chin like he had a beard. Had he shaved it for her? "He'll be here in two days. That'll be Wednesday. I have to remind myself what day it is sometimes. How is it you know about ice deliveries when you were raised in a saloon?"

"I told you, until I was about ten, we lived in a house, and Mama took care of us. She taught me to cook and bake and how a household works. She said I would need it to make a good wife. After she died is when everything changed." Her voice caught in her throat and she looked down at her hands. A gambler's hands. Good for dealing cards but not much else in a long time. "I look forward to being a good wife to you."

"I'm sorry. I shouldn't have pried."

"No. You should know about me. As to the ice, I want to buy some meat for a couple of days and not have it spoil."

He nodded. "But I wouldn't get too much meat, if I were you."

"I thought I'd pick up enough for two dinners with leftovers for lunch the following day."

He lifted a shoulder. "That sounds good."

She finished lunch and got her shawl from her bag. "We're ready."

"Do you really think you'll need the shawl?"

"As you said yourself, it can be cold at this altitude. It's not much higher than Virginia City and I always wore a shawl at night there.."

He nodded. "We're just over eighty-five-hundred feet above sea level almost two-thousand feet higher than Virginia City."

She lifted an eyebrow. "Aren't you just a fount of information today?"

Laughing, he started toward the barn. "I think we should take the buggy. This first trip is bound to be more than I can or want to carry up here."

Addie waited while Douglas hitched the horses to the buggy. Then she set Emmy on the floor of the conveyance while Douglas helped her into it. She picked up the baby and then sat.

Douglas climbed in beside her, and they headed to the town below. He pulled the buggy in front of the general store, facing down the hill, and set the brake. Then he got out and held Emmy while Addie climbed down on her own.

Addie preferred exiting the buggy by herself, as she was more stable. She'd get in that way, too, if Douglas would let her. Those little steps were hard to navigate with just one hand. If anything, Douglas *helping* her was actually more dangerous than if she climbed up on her own. Inside the store she was glad to see it was quite large and well-stocked. She'd never done much shopping except for fripperies and scents, but this store seemed to have more items than the one in Virginia City.

Douglas guided her with a hand to her waist to the register halfway down the same wall as the entry. "Ed Davis, I'd like you to meet my wife Adeline."

The man wore spectacles and his graying hair was slicked down and parted in the middle. She didn't know how he could do it, but his white apron was still pristine after working in the store. He held out his hand. "Pleased to meet you Mrs. Latimer."

"And I you, Mr. Davis. Please, call me Addie. Mrs. Latimer is so formal and I can see this is not a formal town,."

Ed laughed. "No, ma'am. Central City is not formal at all. We have about twenty-four hundred people now. Ten years ago the town was wall to wall people and probably ninety-eight percent of those were miners, mostly men. I'm always happy to see a lovely lady such as yourself, move to our fair city. You look around and if you have any questions, just let me know."

"I will. Thank you, Ed."

He hooked his thumbs into the top of his full-length apron. "Anything for Douglas's wife."

She looked up at Douglas who had the good grace to flush.

"Good to know."

Douglas placed his hand on the back of her waist. "Come my dear. Let's get this shopping done so we can go to the butcher next door." He led her away from Ed.

"Anything for Douglas's wife? You are well known around here."

He sighed. "Of course, I am. I'm one of the largest employers in town."

"I guess I didn't realize that. I don't remember Josiah saying much more than he owned a mine. You live rather modestly."

"Josiah and I weren't always the success we are now…er…I am now. We had to live modestly until we both could finally afford to build homes here and Josiah's is much larger than mine."

"Have you gone to Josiah's house to check if it is still intact? Someone could have gone through all his papers looking for," she shook her head. "I don't know. Something worth killing him for." She looked through the canned goods and picked up several different varieties of fruits for pies. Vegetables would give their meals more variety. She also picked up ten pounds of potatoes. "Do you have a cellar?"

He shook his head. "No, just the pantry. This ground is hard and it's difficult to dig. As to Josiah's house I haven't been to check it out. It just felt wrong to be going through his things, but I will. You can help if you want to."

Addie held Emmy in one arm and placed a ten-pound bag of pinto beans in the bag Douglas held with the other. "I'd be glad to help you. I don't know what I'd be looking for. You might want to take that to the counter."

He shrugged. "I don't either." He took the bag to Ed and returned with it empty.

"Maybe we can do that as a project for tomorrow. What are your working hours?"

"I make my own hours, especially since I've been caring for Emmy. Usually I'm there from eight o'clock to six o'clock. Why?"

"I just wondered when you might like dinner. I have to get the dry laundry in when we get home and put away these groceries before I prepare dinner. Do you have a request? Might as well tell me now since we're here."

"I'd like pork chops with mashed potatoes and gravy, green beans and fresh bread."

She laughed. "Well, I did ask. If you want bread tonight, we need to stop at the bakery. I don't have the time to bake, but I'll make some tomorrow. We'll get pork chops at the butcher, if he has pork, and get the rest here. Let's refill this bag."

Addie went up and down each aisle directing Douglas to put things in the bag. When it got too heavy, he took it to the counter and unloaded it before coming back.

She found everything she wanted and was pleased with the prices.

"That's everything except the flour and sugar. I want a fifty-pound bag of flour and twenty pounds of sugar."

"I'll tell Ed. Do you want to go next door and look at the meat? I'll join you in a moment."

"I think I will. See you soon."

Addie left the general store and she and Emmy went next door to the butcher. While she looked at the offerings a man came in.

"So you're the woman Josiah was supposed to marry? Douglas married you instead, so I hear and I guess I hear right since you have his brat."

"Sir, I don't know who you are, nor do I care to. My daughter is not a brat and I'd appreciate it if you would keep your comments to yourself."

A bell rang as the door opened and Douglas came in. He smiled at Addie and then his face changed. His eyes narrowed, his lips formed a flat line. She could tell he was not happy.

"What are you doing here accosting my wife, Cassidy?"

"Who said I was accosting her? We were simply having a conversation."

Addie stepped toward Douglas. "We were not having a conversation. You were being a bore, and I asked you to keep your comments to yourself."

He waved a hand in the air. "Semantics, my dear."

She felt the tension. "I am—"

"She is not your dear. She is not your anything. Stay away from my family."

Cassidy lifted his shoulders, his hands open flat, palm up in front of him. "Of course. Never let it be said that I forced my attentions on an unwilling woman."

Douglas's right fist landed with a sickening crunch against Cassidy's nose.

The man fell to the floor.

Addie held Emmy close to protect her.

"Now gentlemen, please. Take it outside." The overweight, balding man, came around the counter.

Addie assumed he was the proprietor.

Douglas held his fists up as if to fight. "You want more? Go near my wife again and you'll get more."

"You'll regret this, Latimer." Cassidy held his bloody nose, got to his feet and left the butcher shop.

"Well, that was quite a way to *break* up a boring afternoon." She grinned. "Seriously, wasn't that a bit of an overreaction to his comments?" *I don't want a husband who has a hair-trigger temper.*

"I have my reasons," said Douglas curtly. Then more gently, "He bothered Elizabeth with his unwanted attentions. I won't let that happen to you."

"In that case, thank you. I was afraid you had a bad temper, but I can understand your reaction, now."

She had more questions to ask him, but would wait until they had privacy to voice her concerns.

The butcher turned to them, as though nothing had happened. "What can I get you folks?"

"Horace Pflugner, this is my wife Adeline. She'll be buying our meat from now on. Just put it on my bill."

"Of course. Pleased to meet you, Adeline."

"And you, Horace. Please call me Addie."

He nodded. "As you wish, though Adeline is a lovely German name."

"Thank you for the compliment, kind sir. Douglas, I've seen some very nice pork chops, and I thought I'd get a roast of beef." She turned to her husband. "Will that be acceptable?"

Douglas nodded and put a hand on the back of her waist. "Of course. I'd get four pork chops. I can eat at least two by myself."

She held Emmy with both arms but looked up while thinking. "Well, if I'm planning on having them for lunch the next day, I'd best get six of the chops, Horace, and that nice beef rib roast."

Horace pointed at Addie. "Ah, a woman that has a keen eye for meat. The rib roast is one of the most tender, but because it can be fatty, most women pass it by. Don't worry. I'll trim this piece real nice for you."

Douglas retrieved the meat.

Addie turned to Horace. "Goodbye and be assured you'll be seeing lots more of me.".

Douglas loaded the buggy with their purchases and headed them back home.

"Who was that man who accosted me?"

"Robert Cassidy. He has a mine across the valley from ours. He was trying to talk Josiah into selling, but he'd have none of it. Josiah was waiting for you. He wanted to start a family and settle down. He never would have sold to Cassidy."

Poor Josiah. He wanted so little, a family, and was taken from Earth much too soon. "How's your hand?"

"Fine." He flexed his fingers.

She saw the blood on his knuckles. "I assume the blood does not belong to you."

"Correct. It's his."

"You seem angry still. What aren't you telling me?" *I wonder what has him so worked up he would physically assault another man?*

CHAPTER FIVE

*A*ddie waited for Douglas to get control of his anger before he spoke.

"I think Elizabeth was having an affair with Cassidy. We fought about it the night she ran out and ended up at the mine."

"I thought you believed she and Josiah—never mind."

"That night, all of our dirty laundry was aired."

Addie put a hand on Douglas's knee. "I'm sorry. I can promise you, I take my vows very seriously. I will never be unfaithful to you, just as I expect you to never cheat on me." She squeezed his knee. "Because, if you ever do, I'll shoot you and her, too."

Douglas smiled. "Then I'll be sure to always be true to you. I have no desire to leave Emmy without a father."

Addie wrapped her shawl over her shoulder on one side and made sure Emmy was well bundled, too. The air had taken a decided chill and the time wasn't long before she'd have to start wearing a coat.

At home Addie took Emmy in the house and put her in her crib. When she came back out, a young, brown-haired boy was talking to Douglas, moving his hands very quickly through the air and pointing toward his house.

She walked over to them. "What's the matter?" She feared the worst. She'd seen Joe's type before. Drunk and mean. Alastair only drank when he wasn't playing and since he was either playing or sleeping, she didn't have to deal directly with a drunk. But she'd seen her friend Angel beat up a few times, usually by Ike, the bartender at the Red Dolly saloon.

"Joey says his father came home drunk and beat up his mother because she didn't have dinner on the table. When she told him there was nothing to fix, he flew into a rage and beat her then he ran out of the house. Joey says his mother is on the kitchen floor and won't get up."

Addie turned to go inside. "Did you say she was expecting?"

"Yes and with her not getting up, I fear for the baby. Get Emmy. We can't leave her here."

"Of course not, I'll be right back."

Douglas was right to fear.

Edna Smith, a small, pitifully thin woman, was standing when they arrived surrounded by four children, as blonde as she was, Addie saw the bloodstain on Edna's skirt. She was losing her baby.

Douglas turned to Addie. "I need to take her to the doctor. Will you stay with the children?"

Addie nodded. "I'll bring the children to the house with me, then I can lay Emmy in her crib." She looked down at the baby who was half asleep. "She needs her nap."

He picked up Edna in his arms, carrying her to the buggy which was still hitched up.

Addie feared for their mother but hoped she was a strong woman. These children did not need to be parentless. "Children, come over to my house. Let's get you something to eat and we'll get to know each other. I'm Addie, Douglas's wife and Emmy's new mama."

She led the kids to the house and sat them at the table. She knew they were hungry, but all she had ready was cookies and milk. That would have to do for the time being.

She took Emmy to her room and put her back to bed.

When she returned to the kitchen, Addie poured them all glasses of milk, except the youngest child. For her she poured the milk into one of Emmy's bottles and let her have that. The molasses cookies she'd purchased at the general store were a big hit.

She put a big skillet on the stove, stoked the fire and while the pan heated she beat the rest of their eggs from that morning. Addie scrambled a dozen eggs with ham and added the bread from their shopping trip and butter.

"While this is cooking, why don't you tell me your names and ages? My name is Addie."

The brown-haired boy spoke first. "I'm Joey, and I'm ten."

Then the oldest blonde-haired sister. "I'm Claire, and I'm nine."

"I Larry." Shouted the youngest boy. "I five."

"Larry," said Addie. "There is no need to shout."

"Oh, he always yells everything. Mama has tried everything to make him quit, but he won't," shrugged Joey.

Claire introduced the smallest three girls. She put her hand on top of the oldest. "This is Sara and she's four, then there's Rami, she's three and Audrey in the high chair, she's just one a week ago."

"Thank you. I'll do my best to remember your names, but you may need to help me if I forget."

Joey nodded. "We can do that."

Addie continued to cook the meal. When it was ready, she served it to the kids.

They ate all of it, like they were starving, and she wondered if they weren't.

She heard the door open. *Douglas must be back.*

Addie heard furniture being run in to and it sounded like someone was overturning the chairs. *That couldn't be Douglas.*

Then she heard, cussing and looked at the children.

They were all wide-eyed.

The little ones began to cry.

Joey and his oldest sister tried to comfort the smaller ones.

She guessed, based on the children's fear, that the person stumbling around, cussing and grunting, was their father. Joe Smith.

"Where's my wife?" Joe Smith, with his hair sticking out all over like it had never seen a comb and even from ten feet away she saw his bloodshot eyes and good God, the smell. He stank like stale beer and whiskey and she doubted he'd had a bath in months. He stumbled into the kitchen.

"Douglas took her to the doctor." Addie pointed at the door to the outside. "Get out of my house. You're not welcome here." *Why did I forget to lock the doors? I've been raised in saloons and always locked my door for just this reason. What was I thinking?*

"Those are my kids and you're feeding them right

nice. I guess you can just feed me, too, since Mr. High and Mighty Latimer took my wife."

"Get out of my house, Mr. Smith. Now." She knew not to let him get too close. She lifted her skirt and pulled her gun. "That's far enough. If you take another step, you won't be able to hold a hand of cards." *I will protect these children at all costs.*

"You shouldn't oughta threaten your betters, missy." He stumbled forward, hands out as though to strangle her.

Addie fired and shot his right hand. Her ears were ringing from the noise and burnt gunpowder permeating through the kitchen.

Smith screamed and held his bleeding right hand with his left hand. He backed up. "You bitch."

The children screamed.

Addie heard Emmy crying in the bedroom. *She'll have to wait. She's safe where she's at.*

She knew it would be difficult to see their father shot, but she was taking no chances with their safety. She didn't shift her gaze from Smith. The kids would have to wait.

"Get out of my house or you won't take another breath."

"I'm leaving but I'll be back. I'll get even, you just wait and see."

She followed and locked the back door behind him. Then ran to the living room and locked that door.

She returned to the kitchen to check on the kids. Emmy would just have to wait a moment longer.

When their father was gone, the youngest kids except the baby crowded around her, crying. She raised her skirt and holstered her gun, then dropped to her knees, holding the little ones in her embrace. Her heart pounded in her chest as she was sure the children's were, too. *These children were never going back to that man. Not ever as long as I can help it.*

Joey and Claire were still a bit standoffish and didn't want to be hugged by a stranger.

She understood that and rose. "Claire and Joey, I know you're upset but will you take care of your siblings? I must get Emmy."

Several hours later, Douglas came home through the kitchen where Addie was having a cup of tea. He was alone, and he was pale.

She looked up and around him. "Douglas? Where is Edna? Did the doctor keep her?"

He walked over to her, pulled her into his arms and held her tight. Then he buried his face in her hair. "She died, Addie. The blows he gave her caused her to hemorrhage and the doctor couldn't do anything about it."

Her legs nearly collapsed. If not for Douglas

holding her, she would have. "Oh, my God. Douglas, I'm so sorry." She pulled away so she could look at him. "I'm afraid I did something that will not ease your burden. I shot Smith tonight. He came into the house, and didn't heed my warning. I had no choice." *Maybe I should have shot him more seriously, then he couldn't run from the sheriff.*

As long as you and the kids are okay, nothing else matters." He looked toward the living room. "Are they here?"

"Yes, they're all in the living room, playing."

"Good. They are not to go with their father under any circumstances. I just spent the last hour with the sheriff. He's getting the judge to issue a warrant for Joe Smith for murder in the death of Edna Smith."

"What should I do if he returns, thinking to take his kids?"

"They can't go with him, no matter what. Joey may want to. The man is his father and a boy often feels like he needs a father regardless of how insane or dangerous the man is."

"I had Joey and Claire, the two oldest, get their clothes and bring them over here. Their mother's clothing, too. They each had basically what they were wearing with a second pair of drawers."

"We'll need to buy them clothes. The mercantile has clothing. Joyce, the owner, will be able to help you with sizes. Since the kids are growing you should get clothes that are bigger than what they are wearing now so they can grow into them."

"Sounds like a good idea. We'll take the kids tomorrow. For now, I'm putting that roast I got into the oven. We'll feed them a good meal tonight and then when we're out with them I'll do some more grocery shopping. I'm afraid you'll have to come with us. I can't drive the buggy."

He nodded. "I'll do that. I want to leave first thing though. I need to go to the mine and see how the clearing is going."

"All right. I'll get up early and gather the eggs. Joey can help me by milking the cow. You'll need to take care of Emmy or I'll take care of Emmy and you can help Joey with the morning chores."

Douglas put an arm around her shoulders. "You're a great mother, taking on these kids and Emmy without any complaint. I'll help Joey. We'll give those two chores to him later on. He'll appreciate being needed."

These events were so much more than what she was prepared for. She felt her eyes fill with tears, but she would not let them fall. Addie had to be a mother now, not just to Emmy but to the six Smith children.

She enjoyed Douglas's arm on her and wanted to lean into him, but she caught herself just in time. "Thank you for the compliment. I try to do my best. I was an only child so I'm glad these kids have each other. Now if you'll take care of Emmy, I'll get to cooking and baking."

He gave her a squeeze before releasing her.

She felt bereft at the loss of his arm.

"Baking?"

She nodded. She'd unpacked and put away all the groceries while he'd been gone. They would return the boxes next trip and have them refilled. "I'm trying to make a loaf of bread before dinner. I'm not sure how successful I'll be so I'll make biscuits as well. The children will enjoy them with some of the canned fruit I bought today."

"Understood. I'll talk to Joey about helping with the chores." He left the kitchen.

Addie prepared the roast for the oven first. As for the groceries she hadn't been sure where everything was supposed to go so she decided to put the food away as she saw fit. She found the bins for flour and sugar. She'd need more of both very quickly with so many mouths to feed, but she hoped the children would start to put on some weight.

Douglas seemed very loving—placing his arm around her shoulders and then giving her the compliment. She wondered if that was for her or for the mother she was becoming.

She went to find Claire and found her with the younger children in the living room. "Claire, may I speak to you please?"

"Sure."

The girl was nine and it was time she learned how to cook. Addie was just the person to teach her.

She pulled Claire aside. "I'd like for you to start helping me in the kitchen. Would you like that?"

The smile that split the girl's face was blinding. "Oh, yes, ma'am. I'd very much like to learn how to cook. Mama never seemed to have time and we usually didn't have much food."

"That's changing right now. We're preparing tonight's dinner. Tomorrow we'll fix scrambled eggs again and then go to the mercantile for more groceries and new clothes for all of you. How does that sound?"

The smile she gave Addie wasn't quite as big. "Wonderful."

Addie put her arm around the girl's slim shoulders. She felt every bone and shuddered at the way these children were treated. "I sense something is wrong. What is it?"

"We've been promised new clothes before."

"Let me guess, by your father."

The girl nodded, her eyes filling with tears. "But we never got them."

"Well, I'm not your father and I always keep my word. I will never lie to you and I expect the same from you in return. Okay?"

Claire nodded. "Oh, yes, ma'am."

Addie squeezed the girl's shoulders. "Let's get dinner started, shall we?"

"Yes, ma'am."

How in the world did this family survive until now?

All the children sat at the table.

She and Douglas stood at the head of the table, she with her hands clasped in front of her.

Douglas cleared his throat. "Children, as much as it pains me to tell you this, I must. Your mother died tonight from injuries she sustained from the beating by your father. I'm very sorry."

Claire broke into tears and the smaller ones ran to her and cried because she did, for they were too young to fully understand that their mother would never be home again.

Joey stood off to one side, his mouth in a flat line and his hands in fists at his side. Addie knew that look. It was anger, though she didn't know if it was at his father for killing his mother or at his mother for dying. He turned and ran out of the house.

Addie touched Douglas's arm. "Go after him."

He shook his head. "Joey needs to be alone to process his grief…and his anger. There is nothing I can do to help him right now."

She let out a breath. "I suppose you're right. I felt the same way when my mother died. I was so angry at her for leaving me and even though I knew my father didn't kill her, I resented him for still being alive."

He nodded. "I was the same when my mother died."

Douglas looked toward the door Joey left through. "He's probably gone to the barn or maybe home, but he'll be back."

"I hope so."

The roast she'd gotten for her and Douglas was barely enough for the eight them. The children ate everything put in front of them.

The bread didn't get done for dinner but would be perfect for tomorrow morning. She'd start more then, plus she'd bake a cake.

Addie realized raising seven children would take a lot more of her time than she'd planned for. Thankfully, Claire was thrilled to help and to learn. Soon she'd be making the bread on her own and then Addie would teach her how to bake other things.

After dinner, the children seemed to be waiting for her to tell them what to do, which only made sense. "If you all would go into the living room, we'll get sleeping arrangements made and then you can get ready for bed."

"We can do that." Joey put his arms around Larry. The boys seemed to gravitate to one another.

Claire put her arms around Sara and Rami who hung onto her skirt. "Shh, now," she soothed them. "You're okay."

Addie went to Emmy's room.

She picked up her daughter.

The baby cried but her cries subsided the closer Addie held her. "Oh, sweetie, I'm so sorry. Yes, Mama's sorry. She didn't forget you. You were sleeping so well."

When Emmy was only sniffling, they joined the Smith children in the living room.

"I know it's been a very hard day for you all, but I want you to make your beds now. If Joey and Claire will come with me, we'll find blankets. I think the three youngest can sleep crosswise on the small bed in Emmy's room. Audrey can share Emmy's crib. Claire and Joey, if you curl up, with your heads at the opposite ends of the sofa, you can sleep there. That's the best I can do at the moment. You'll be staying here for the foreseeable future."

Claire spoke up. "I'll help you if you'll show me where the blankets are. I'll make up the sofa for me and Joey."

"Well, since I only arrived today, I don't know.

We'll have to ask Douglas. He's still in the kitchen. I'll be right back."

Douglas sat hunched at the table over a cup of coffee.

"Where are the blankets?"

"What? Oh, there are two on the shelf above the rod in the master closet."

"Thank you. I'll get them."

Addie returned to the living room. "Claire, would you hold Emmy while I get the blankets?"

The girl grinned. "I'd love, to."

Addie returned with the blankets.

Claire passed Emmy back to Addie and made the sofa into a bed for her and Joey.

She couldn't get our of her head the picture in the master bedroom. A huge portrait of a beautiful blonde woman. *Elizabeth.* It couldn't be anyone else. She wasn't sure how well she'd sleep with Elizabeth looking down at her.

CHAPTER SIX

The following day Robert Cassidy sat in the office at his mine and touched his broken nose. He vowed Douglas Latimer would pay for it. But first he needed Josiah's will. He had to destroy it and then he would destroy Douglas and the mine would be his. The widow wouldn't be able to hang on to it and would be glad to sell it to him. Or perhaps he'd marry her. He saw through her irritated attitude yesterday. She had to be that way because of Douglas, but he knew she was attracted to him. All women were.

Elizabeth was. She was angry when I told her we were through. She'd had a fight with Douglas and came to me for solace. I had none to give. I was done with her, so she went to Josiah.

Robert was sad that she'd died, she was a good

bedmate even after having that brat that Douglas fawned over. Oh well, upsetting things happened sometimes, but he would carry on with his plans. Nothing would come between him and Douglas's Old Glory mine.

---

*D*ouglas loaded everyone up in his surrey and they went to town to get the children new clothes. Neither Addie nor Douglas told the children what they were doing and why everyone had to go to town.

He pulled up in front of mercantile and everyone went inside. Douglas left their surrey parked in front of the store.

"Douglas." A pretty woman in her early fifties greeted him. "Who do we have here?" She walked up to Addie. "You must be Douglas's new wife. I'm Joyce and I'm very pleased to meet you. And all the Smith children. Hello, kids. What can I do for you all today?"

"Hi, I'm Addie. Very nice to make your acquaintance. We're here to get these children new clothes. What do you have that might fit them?"

"Oh my, that's wonderful." She looked up at Douglas. "Why don't you take the boys and see what you can find? I'll take the girls right over here. I don't have a lot, but we should be able to get them each a couple of sets of garments."

Addie followed Joyce with Claire, Emmy, Audrey, Rami and Sara.

Douglas took Joey and Larry with him to the boy's clothes.

The store was quite large but even so, the choice in clothing was limited. They ended up finding two sets of new clothes for each child, plus undergarments and nightgowns and pajamas.

"Can we get candy sticks for everyone?" Addie asked Douglas.

"I don't know why not. The children have been especially good today."

Addie began looking at the colorful jars of stick candy sitting on the counter. "You've got so many choices," she told Joyce.

"We have something for everyone," the store owner said with a little puff of her chest.

"Kids, you can each get a stick of candy. What flavors would you like?"

Shouts came from each child. "Cherry, strawberry, peppermint, orange."

Addie laughed. "Looks like you better give us two of every flavor, Mrs. Davis."

Douglas paid for all their purchases and the family, now including the Smith children, headed home.

One week later, after they'd gotten the Smith children feeling safe and comfortable with them, Addie called Claire and Joey to join her. "Claire. Joey. Douglas and I must leave you for a little while today. We need to go to Josiah's house and look for some important documents. I don't want to leave you alone but circumstances dictate otherwise. I need you both to care for the younger children while we are gone. Can you do that? I also want you to stay inside, lock the doors and don't let anyone in. Understand? No one, not even your father."

Claire spoke up first. "I understand and will make sure everything is locked up and we won't answer the door." She looked over at her brother. "Will we, Joey?"

Joey's mouth was in a flat line. He obviously didn't like the idea of keeping his father out.

Addie looked at Joey. "Well?"

"All right. I won't open the door for anyone."

Putting her hand on Joey's shoulder, she gave it a squeeze. "I know this is hard for you, but it is necessary to ensure your safety and that of your siblings."

He gave a single nod of his head.

Addie decided that was good enough and would be all she'd get from him, it was a promise.

A short time later she and Douglas left for Josiah's home.

She saw he carried a burlap bag.

Addie didn't like to leave Emmy for long so she hoped they could find what Josiah was killed for quickly. Her hopes were dashed when she entered the house and found it had been ransacked, as she feared.

Her shoulders slumped. "How are we supposed to find anything in this mess? What are we looking for anyway?"

"We're looking for Josiah's will. He had a safe installed for important documents. Come with me."

She looked at each room, thinking about which child would best fit the space. Six bedrooms would be perfect for their growing family.

He led the way to the last bedroom on the right.

The room had only a bed and a dresser. The mattress was on the floor, slit open.

Douglas walked to the closet and went down on his knees. He knocked on the floor until the hollow sound stopped. He pulled up four of the thin slats of wood exposing a combination safe in the floor.

He proceeded to open the safe.

There had to be ten-thousand dollars in cash. Under that was a large bag of gold. She'd never seen so much money in her life. *Even when Alastair was way up, he'd never had more than five-thousand dollars. Why in the world didn't Josiah use a bank?*

Then there were the documents. Many documents

Addie and Douglas both began sorting through the papers.

"Douglas, I found his will."

"Good. We need to find out if that is what the person, who I believe is Robert Cassidy, wanted."

She handed him the multi-page will.

Douglas opened it and began to read. His eyebrows rose as he read.

"What? What is it?"

"Listen to this. 'I, Josiah Colter, being of sound mind and body, do hereby leave all my worldly goods to Miss Adeline Brady, my fiancée. Should she predecease me then Douglas Latimer will receive everything.' Then he's listed his assets. There are many more than even I was aware of."

Addie needed to sit and went to the bed, sitting on the wooden frame. "He left everything to me? But why? We weren't even married yet. Heavens, we hadn't even met. I don't understand."

Douglas shrugged. "I don't either, but it is what it is. You own half of The Old Glory mine."

She got up and walked to him, placing a hand on his arm. "I'm sorry, Douglas. I know it's not what you wanted, but at least we're married now and what I have is yours."

He stood, standing by the safe, and turned to her. "I didn't marry you because of the mine. I didn't know what Josiah had in his will. I married you because it was the right thing to do, for Emmy...and for me, too."

She gazed down at their feet, unsure of where else to look.

He lifted her chin with a knuckle until she was looking at him. He lowered his head and put his lips on hers.

She wrapped her arms around his neck and kissed him back...with love? Was a week too short a time to say she was in love with her husband? Probably, but the circumstance was what it was. "I know we shouldn't but I want you to make love to me, Douglas. I see a bed there. All we have to do is lay the mattress back on the frame."

He made short work of returning the mattress to the slatted frame of the large wood bed. The headboard and footboard were carved with elaborate designs that looked to her like a woodland scene. Deer, rabbits and squirrels frolicked in front of large Ponderosa pine trees.

Addie spread the sheet, which had been abandoned in a pile on the floor, over the mattress. Then she unbuttoned her blouse and its sleeves. She undid the button on her skirt letting it fall to the floor, followed by her chemise and bloomers.

Douglas removed all of his clothes, too. He walked to her and tucked a loose strand of hair behind an ear. "You're beautiful. Maybe the loveliest woman I've ever seen."

"You don't have to flatter me. I'm married to you, remember?"

"It's not flattery if it's true." He leaned down and kissed her, picking her up in his arms and taking her to the bed and laying her in the middle. He lay beside her, propped up on an elbow. "What do you know of making love?"

She loved the feel of his skin next to hers. The way his hard planes fit with her soft curves. The sparse hair on his chest tickled her side and she smiled. "I know the basics of how we go together, but little else."

"I'm starting with pleasuring you. You'll enjoy it, and in the process I will ready you for me."

He did exactly as he said he would. She felt wonderful, and yet, something was missing.

She needn't have worried. Douglas proceeded to make sweet love to her, taking great care of her.

After coming back to her senses and having cuddled with Douglas for a short time, Addie lifted her head and gazed at her husband, who was now her husband in fact as well as in name. "We must go home. The children will wonder where we are."

Douglas kissed the top of her head. "You're right. I don't want them afraid we have abandoned them."

Addie dressed quickly.

Douglas did the same. He took the burlap bag he brought and put everything from the safe into the bag.

She followed him out to the buggy. As they rode home, she said her thoughts out loud. "I'll come back and clean up the place. I'm hoping to leave Joey and Claire in charge of their younger siblings and Emmy. But I want to see if they have both proved they can handle the responsibility."

"All right. I'll drop you in the morning on the way to the mine. I'll be there for a couple of hours. I could pick you up on the way back home."

"That sounds perfect. It will take me at least that long to put things to rights in Josiah's house." She paused and clasped her hands together. "Douglas, I'm wondering if maybe we should move into it, into Josiah's house. It's so much bigger than our house. It has six bedrooms. Josiah told me in his letters he wanted lots of children."

Douglas swatted the horses' butts with the reins. "He did. He too was an only child but he was raised in an orphanage. He was determined none of his children would ever go through that."

"I understand. I wouldn't want that for any of my children either." She placed a hand on his knee and looked up at him. "So what do you think of moving in there?"

He didn't even hesitate. "I think it's a great idea. I'll have the judge, a friend of mine, authenticate the will. We shouldn't need an attorney. Then we can take possession. I'd been thinking the same thing myself but wasn't sure how you would take it. Even though there is more room, some of the kids will still need to double up. They are used to that, and I think it would be best to keep them together, at least the little ones. Whatever makes them feel comfortable is what we'll try to do."

Addie smiled wide. "I think I could kiss you."

"Well, what's stopping you?" He put the reins in his left hand and placed his right arm around her shoulders, bringing her close.

She put her arms around his neck and pressed herself against his hard chest before she pulled his head down for her kiss. With her tongue circling his, she tasted him and put all her love into the kiss. Did he feel it? Did he feel how much she loved him?

Douglas finally pulled back and then rubbed his thumb along her lower lip. "I'm tempted to turn around and make love to you again, but it's too soon. You've been so exhausted, even though you said you wanted me to. You have immediately fallen asleep in my arms every night since we got the children. That was your first time and you need to recover. Tomorrow night though, all bets are off."

Addie giggled. She shook her head at herself but she felt light as a schoolgirl on her first outing with her first beau. Actually, he was her second beau.

Josiah had been first, technically speaking, since she was to marry him. But Douglas was first on every other level.

Still she couldn't believe she'd just giggled. She left her arm through the crook in his elbow and leaned into him, resting her head against his shoulder. "I can't wait until tomorrow night." And she meant every word.

Douglas let her off by the kitchen door and then took the animals to the barn to care for them.

Addie used her key to go inside. Upon entering, she smelled food cooking.

Claire stood in front of the stove stirring something.

Addie sniffed the air again. "What smells so good?"

"Dinner. It's bean soup. It's the only thing I know how to make without a recipe." Claire put down the spoon onto a ceramic spoon holder.

"Well, it smells wonderful. What do you say we bake cornbread to go with the beans?"

The girl's eyes lit up. "I've wanted to learn."

"Are the beans ready to simmer?"

"Oh, yes, they've been simmering for almost an hour. I can leave them long enough to learn how to make the cornbread."

"First melt some butter in two skillets."

Claire did as asked.

Claire stirred the pot of bean soup a couple of times to keep the bottom from burning. "It's ready now, but it'll simmer and be good whenever the cornbread is done."

The child was thrilled with the results of her first effort. The cornbread was light, golden brown around the edges and smelled wonderful.

Addie put an arm around Claire's shoulders. "I'd say you did very well. Thank you for making dinner. Now I need to check on the other children."

The door opened and Douglas entered, locking the door behind him.

"Something smells terrific." He looked at Claire. "Have you been cooking? I do remember Edna was a good cook before she got sick."

Addie gave Douglas a kiss. "I'll check on the other children."

He shook his head. "Let me. I need some Emmy time anyway."

Addie lifted her brows. "I understand that feeling. You go on."

"See you ladies at dinner."

Addie gazed at the little girl.

Claire shuffled her feet. "I wasn't sure you were coming back. You seemed to be gone for a long time."

Addie's mouth turned down and she closed her eyes for a moment. She should never have asked

Douglas to make love to her. Claire's mother was only dead a week and Addie was already being a bad mother.

Walking over to the table with her arm around Claire's shoulders, Addie sat and had the girl sit, too. "Claire, we will always come back. We would never take you in and then abandon you. Understand?"

The child shrugged and looked up, tears filling her eyes. "Mama left and didn't come back."

Addie kissed her forehead. "That's different. Your mother passed away. Your father killed her. She would never have left you otherwise."

"I hate my father. I would kill him if I could." The child whispered the statement.

"I understand and I don't blame you. I feel the same way."

Claire swiped at her eyes with the back of her hand. She lifted her chin just a little and her blonde brows crinkled. "Joey says the sheriff will arrest our father if he catches him and he'll be hung for killing Mama. Is that true?"

Addie wanted to soften the truth but couldn't and still be honest with Claire. "Yes, it is."

"My father is an evil man."

She squeezed the girl's shoulders. Even though Claire was only nine, she'd proven herself in many ways. "That is my belief, too."

Joey rounded the corner of the kitchen. His back

stiff and his hands in fists. "How can you say that? Claire, he's our father."

Claire stood and turned to her brother and put her hands on her hips. "He killed Mama. He always left us hungry and wanting when he could have taken care of us and loved us. We were nothing more than someone to do his bidding when he was around. He is an evil man and you know it."

Joey stood across from her and shouted. "What does that make us, if he's so evil?"

"Lucky we took after Mama!" Claire shouted back, her chest heaving.

Joey swiped at the tears on his cheeks. He looked at Addie.

She held open her arms. She could only imagine what these children had been through in their young lives. There should be laws against this treatment of children by anyone, their parents included, but she knew they, like their mothers, were chattel owned by their fathers. Unfortunately, she couldn't help all the children in the world, but she could help these six.

Joey ran into her arms.

Addie wrapped him in her embrace. "It's all right. You're a good boy. You're not your father." She looked up at Claire and lifted an arm toward her.

Claire also hurried to her and hugged Joey.

Holding the two children, trying to ease their

fears, Addie hugged them tightly. "You're part of my family, now."

"Our family," said Douglas entering the kitchen, carrying Emmy, and coming over to the little group. He knelt on the floor and wrapped his arm around them all. "You are members of our family now and don't you forget it."

"Yes, sir," said Joey.

Claire nodded.

Addie knew the children had a great fear of being left and Addie should have realized that before asking Douglas to make love to her. She was wrong. So very wrong.

Losing their mother and father so close together had scarred them. She and Douglas would have to remind them often of their love for them and the children's status in the family. Would they overcome their fears and believe her and Douglas?

CHAPTER SEVEN

*A*ddie paced the kitchen waiting for Douglas. He was talking to the judge about Josiah's will. She didn't want to make any plans until she was sure they could legally move into the house.

The back door opened and Douglas walked in and locked the door behind him.

"Well, what did the judge say? Can we move into the house?"

"Calm down." He walked over to her. "The judge, is a friend of mine and Josiah's. He looked over the will and declared it legal and binding. We can move into the house whenever we're ready."

"I'm ready. I want the kids to sleep in real beds and have their own bedrooms, well the older kids anyway. The little ones can still share."

"Whatever you wish. The house is yours."

Addie made Douglas buy new mattresses for every bed in Josiah's house and for the two bedsteads they took from Douglas's home. The younger children preferred to be in one room together so Addie took the largest of the bedrooms, other than the master and put one double and one single bed in the room.

Claire walked inside a bedroom and ran her hand over the Tallboy dresser, around to the bureau and finally the pretty brass bed. She grinned from ear to ear. "This is my room? All by myself?"

Addie nodded.

Joey narrowed his eyes. "What's the catch? I ain't never had my own room either."

Addie put her hands behind her. "There's no catch. You are the oldest of the children and deserve to have your own room. That is a luxury I never had. The way I grew up, after my mama died, I shared a room with my father in whatever saloon we were in, at least until the owner threw us out."

Claire's eyes shot wide. "Really? With your father?"

"Yes. He didn't spend much time in the room, and when he was in it, I left. I'd walk around town with a candy stick until the schoolmarm took pity on me. She taught me to read and write. I even gave up my candy stick so I could learn. But I would eat the candy later. It's my downfall. I like anything sweet. Candy, cookies, cake, pie, whatever. How about you all? I know you like cookies and cake. What else do you like?"

"Everything you said." Joey licked his lips.

"Good. I like to bake, so I'll try to have something for you every day. Claire, you can help me."

The girl smiled. "Thanks. I'd love to learn."

"I'll bring you sheets for your beds. Do you need help with the sheets?"

Joey shook his head.

Claire shook her head, too. "We did most of the housekeeping. Mama was sick a lot of the time with the baby she carried."

Joey looked over at his sister. "She managed to cook, when we had food, but that was about all she could do."

Pointing back and forth between herself and Joey, Claire said, "We had to learn. Mama supervised us the first couple of times and then she lay on the sofa until our father was supposed to be home for dinner. Finally, she put away dinner for him and fed us. I'm not sure she ate very often though."

"When she did eat, most of the time she threw it all backup," said Joey.

Addie's mouth turned down and she lowered her chin. *I hope when I'm expecting I don't do that.* "I'm so sorry. She's out of pain now and can eat anything she wants."

"That's what I hope," said Claire.

Addie looked at Joey, but he didn't say anything, and she wasn't about to push him. In time, he would come to his own beliefs.

After all the children's beds were made, Addie led the way to the kitchen. "I need to scrub this stove, but not too much. I don't think Josiah did much cooking. We however will be doing a lot. I must check to see if Emmy is still sleeping. With the other children playing in their room, it's hard to hear her. I'll be right back."

A few minutes later, Addie returned. "She's still fast asleep. Let's get to work." She went to the four-door icebox. The two doors on top were for ice and the two larger ones below for food. Addie opened one of the large doors and closed it as fast as she could, waving her hand in front of her face. The smell of rotted food permeated the kitchen just from the short time the icebox was open. "Looks like I'm cleaning the icebox before the stove. Joey, bring me a burlap bag and then go light the trash barrel, please. We'll be burning some nasty stuff today."

"Yes, ma'am." He ran outside.

"I can clean the stove while you do the icebox, if you want," said Claire.

Addie shook her head. "I need you to watch the

children and make sure they don't get into trouble. You might want to bring them all into the living room, except Emmy who can stay in her crib, since she's sleeping."

"Okay." Claire headed out to the bedrooms to gather the children.

Addie noticed the slight slumping of her shoulders. *I wanted a family, now I have to learn how to manage one. I think I'll make a list of the chores that must be done every day and who is responsible for doing them.* "Claire, after Joey gets done burning this stuff from the icebox he can watch the kids and you can help me in here."

The girl turned around and perked up. "Really?"

"Yes, really." Addie knew what it was like to want to be near her mom all the time and even though she wasn't Claire's mother…yet…she was the closest person to one.

Joey slammed into the kitchen. "The barrel's lit. I put a piece of wood in it to get it going real good."

"Thank you. I appreciate your help. I'll load up this burlap bag and you can burn it all…bag included. Just give me a few minutes. You might want to go into the living room. The smell will be awful."

"You don't have to tell me twice." He hightailed it out of the room.

Addie took a deep breath and opened the icebox. Things were unrecognizable. Molded, melted and just plain rotten. She quickly started throwing vegetables, meat and butter, crock included, into the bag. When everything was out of the icebox she carried the bag outside and set it by the door.

"Joey! Joey!" she yelled.

"I'm here, Addie. Are you ready for me to take that stuff and burn it? Wow, it stinks in here."

"Yes, burn everything. Dump the bag and then toss it in after the stuff. It's going to smell, so try not to get any on you."

"Okay."

"The bag is just outside the door."

Douglas walked in from the direction of the living room, waving his hand in front of his face. "What is that God-awful smell?"

Addie sighed. "The contents of Josiah's icebox. You can help me by putting on a bucket of water and lighting the stove. I need to clean the icebox and I think Joey will probably need a bath. I can't imagine he won't get something on him as he burns that garbage."

"Sure." He scrunched his nose and put his finger over his nostrils. "If you can handle the odor, then I guess I can, too."

She laughed. "You get used to it and I held my breath as much as possible while I was throwing everything into a burlap bag. Totally disgusting. We should have seen to it sooner, but I didn't even think about it."

"I didn't either, though I doubt if I had, I would have had the fortitude to clean it out like you did. I'd have hired someone."

"If I'd known that was an option..."

"Too late." He came over and took her about the waist. "You already did it." He leaned down and kissed her. "And I thank you for it."

She linked her arms around his neck careful not to touch him with her hands. "You're welcome. I should have it cleaned out shortly, but I haven't cleaned the stove yet. Claire wants to help me with the kitchen and I told her after Joey was done they could switch. He'll watch the kids and she'll help me. Unless you want to relieve her and watch the little ones. You probably should check on Emmy first. I don't hear her, but I don't know if she's not making any noise or I just can't hear her. Claire should be able to hear her though."

"She was awake and Claire was changing her when I came in. She said she'd feed her afterward." He kissed down the side of her neck. "Do you have some sugar for your hardworking husband?"

Addie giggled and gave him a big kiss. She didn't have to wait long for him to take control of the kiss.

He pulled her close and then held her head with his hands.

"Oh, yuck, don't you two do anything besides kiss?" Joey rolled his eyes.

Addie looked at the boy and grinned.

He had his hands on his hips. "I came in to tell you the trash is going real good and stinks to high heaven. The neighbors will wonder what in the heck we're burning."

She looked out at the trash barrel. "Oh, dear."

"I think we'll be going out to dinner tonight," said Douglas. "And we'll open all the windows when we go. Maybe the house will smell better when we return and are ready for bed."

"Yay!!" hollered Joey. "Going out to dinner. We ain't never been out to eat before."

Addie let go of Douglas and turned to Joey. "I expect you all to be on your best behavior."

"And I want all of you to wash your hands and face before we go," added Douglas.

Joey smiled wide. "Oh, yes, ma'am, we will be. I promise." He turned to Douglas. "I'll make sure we all get washed."

Addie nodded. "Good. Now, I want you to relieve Claire of kid duty so she can help me clean the kitchen."

"Okay." He slumped his shoulders and hung his head.

She walked over to the stove and checked the water. It was warm enough for washing up. She gazed over at Joey. "Don't be all hangdog on me. You have to share responsibility for your brother and sisters."

Joey stood a little straighter. "You're right." He marched out of the room.

Addie got a basin from under the sink and ladled some of the warm water into it and washed her hands. When she was drying them, she turned her attention back to Douglas. "I thought you'd be at the mine longer."

"I wasn't needed. My foreman, Woodrow Jones, has everything under control. It looks like you have it all in hand here, too. I'm not needed anywhere." He frowned and hung his head.

She walked back to him. "I'll always need you."

He turned his head and placed kisses along her neck. "I'm glad to hear it." He kissed her lips. "Very glad."

"I'll put you to work if you stay around here."

"Point me where you want me."

"Would you clean all the ashes from the fireplace and make sure the flue opens properly? I don't want to have a fire in there and then fill the house with smoke."

"Your wish is my command."

I wish I knew if you love me, or do you still have a wall around your heart?

After a wonderful dinner at the Toll House, Addie put Emmy and Audrey to bed and made sure the rest of the children were ready for bed and then, in the living room, she read to them from Alice's Adventures in Wonderland by Lewis Carroll. She looked around and all of them seemed to be transfixed.

Addie came to a good stopping point. "Now, children, that's enough for tonight. Go to your rooms and I'll be in directly to tuck you in."

A chorus of "Yes, ma'am" and "Okay" sounded across the living room as the children left.

She went to the kitchen, where Douglas was reading that day's Denver Post newspaper.

"All right. We need to say goodnight, like my mother always did with me."

He set the paper on the table and stood. "Following you."

Addie left and started with the younger children. She tucked them in and then kissed their forehead, doing the same for every child.

Douglas also kissed every child on the forehead.

Joey was the last one they tucked in. When she and Douglas said goodnight to the boy, they slipped out of the room, closing the door behind them as they'd done with all the children.

"Care to retire, m'dear?"

"Oh, yes, sir, Mr. Latimer, sir." She giggled.

Douglas chuckled and placed a hand on her waist, guiding her to their bedroom.

Addie turned back the covers on the bed and then changed into her nightgown. She looked up at the hated portrait of the woman Douglas couldn't forget. Addie couldn't believe he would hang it in their new home.

Douglas eased under the blankets. "I thought we weren't wearing clothes to bed anymore."

"I just thought, with the children in a new house, that it was prudent for one of us to have clothes on should they need us."

"We'd have long enough to don a robe, or in my case pants. Now, take that off and come to bed."

She sighed but admitted to herself she would rather feel his skin next to hers and so removed the gown before crawling in bed next to him.

He held out his arm and then curled it around her shoulders when she was close, drawing her closer. "Now, isn't this better?" She placed her leg over his. "Much, much better."

Addie turned on her side and propped on an elbow. "I'm you to make love to me. I know adding another child to this brood is probably not the best idea, but I need to feel alive. And even though I know it's not the best time to be adding a child, I want to give Emmy brothers and sisters. I don't know if we'll be able to keep the Smith children. They could have aunts or uncles or grandparents that will want to raise them. We wouldn't be able to stop that."

He smoothed her hair. "No, we wouldn't but we can petition the judge to adopt them. Then we'll find out if there are any other relatives."

"I think that's what we should do. The children are comfortable with us, so far and we know what they've been through. I'm becoming more enamored with them as the day passed. They are well-behaved children and deserve to have a chance in life."

"I don't disagree. We'll do the best we can for them."

Addie cuddled closer, placing her left leg and arm across Douglas's body." She was falling in love with her husband. They'd only been married for a week and already, he was showing her what kind of man he was. A good man.

Douglas blew out the lamp and then proceeded to make love to her, much to her delight. At this rate, she'd be expecting in no time…she hoped.

She didn't think she could have gotten luckier in a mate but she wondered if she'd be able to break through the wall around his heart.

CHAPTER EIGHT

Two months later

Addie stood at the stove, stirring the stew for their dinner.

Douglas came into the kitchen from the front of the house, wrapped his arms around her waist and kissed her neck.

"Where are the children?"

"Out playing in the bac yard, except for the babies who are in their crib. Which reminds me. We need to get another crib. Audrey is getting too big to share one with Emmy. Audrey is a fourteen-month old and needs to be in her own bed. Besides, she's walking and wants to be with the other children, which I'm about to let her do. Claire and Joey are good with the younger children and they will keep her safe while she plays with them."

"All right, we'll get another crib. I didn't see one at either the general store or the mercantile, but we have a local carpenter who might. Even if he doesn't, I'm sure I can order one."

She turned in his arms and smiled. "That would be wonderful. That bedroom has plenty of room for two cribs. And, as they get bigger, we'll move out the cribs and two single beds in."

"You're becoming very good at managing our household. These kids love you. I have a surprise for you."

She widened her eyes. "I love surprises…as long as they're good ones."

"This is a good one, mostly."

, his chest. "Well don't keep me in suspense. What is the surprise?"

"I had our attorney file a petition to adopt the Smith children. The only problem is Joe Smith is still alive, as far as we know, and the judge won't grant the petition unless we find Joe Smith or prove that he's dead."

She closed her eyes for a moment and then sighed. "He'll never sign the paperwork giving us his children, even if we could find him."

Douglas narrowed his eyes and his mouth formed

a straight line. "He will if we pay him. I just have to let it be known—"

She sagged in his arms. "You think he'll sell his children?" She shook her head. "I don't think so. Once he realizes he can get money for them, he'll keep coming back for more."

"We don't give him the money until he signs the papers and we don't let him take the children either. If he shows up here, get the sheriff. Probably send Claire. Joey is still too close."

"You think even after watching his father kill his mother, he'll still be tied to the man?"

His eyebrows wrinkled the skin between them as he frowned. "Yes, I'm afraid so. Joey wants a father and I don't think he's accepted me in that role yet."

With her arms around his waist, she laid her head on his chest and hugged him tightly. "He will."

Douglas shrugged, keeping his arms around her. "I don't know if he will or not. I hope he does."

"Let's check on the babies and take Audrey outside to play. Emmy enjoys just watching the kids."

In the babies' bedroom, Audrey stood on one end of the crib bouncing. As soon as she saw Addie, she put up her arms and cried out.

Addie went over and picked her up. "Looks like someone wants to go outside." She sniffed the air. "But first, you need a clean diaper."

Douglas picked up Emmy. "She needs one, too. You take that end of the crib, and I'll take this one."

Together, they made short work of the babies' diapers, tossing the dirty ones in the almost full the bucket by the crib.

"After I give Audrey to her brother or sister, I have to come back in and start water for the diapers. They have to be washed."

"All right. Do you need my help?"

"No. Taking care of Emmy is enough." She leaned up and kissed his cheek. "Thank you."

His eyes widened. "For what? Spending time with my children? That is my pleasure." He kissed Emmy's cheek and then Audrey's.

She pulled back and looked up at him. "Have you come any closer to finding the murderer? What if he's after you next?"

His gaze seemed to be off in the distance. "It doesn't matter. You own half the mine. If I die, you'll inherit the other half. You'll be fine."

She narrowed her eyes, her throat tight. "What kind of answer is that? I don't want to be fine. I want to be married to you. I want you to be alive and well and capable of helping me raise these children and any that we might have."

"Are you—"

She shrugged. "I don't know. Maybe. I need to see the doctor to be sure but I haven't had my menses since we married, three months ago. So it's possible."

He put Emmy into one arm, smiled and hugged Addie to him with the other. "That's wonderful." Then he sobered and the smile left his face.

"Robert wants the mine and has designs on killing you as well. I know he does." She placed a hand on his chest. "Please Douglas, don't work in the mine. Stay in the office, regardless of whatever is said. I don't believe for a moment that Robert doesn't have someone on your payroll actually working for him. Someone who will try to get you into the mine."

He kissed her forehead. "I'll be careful. I promise."

As tears filled her eyes she turned her head and pressed it against his chest. She would not let him see her cry...wouldn't let him know how much she cared...how much she loved him.

Addie knew he didn't feel the same for her. Douglas was still in love with Elizabeth. She knew this because there was that large portrait of her in their bedroom. She'd hoped when they moved into Josiah's house that the portrait would be relegated to the barn or at least to Emmy's room not theirs, but that was not to be. She still had to wake up with that woman looking down at her, smiling smugly at her as though to say, "He'll never love you. He'll always be in love with me."

Just the thought of the painting made her angry. She pulled away from Douglas. "Claire. Come get your sister, please." Addie watched Audrey run to her sister and then at the last minute she'd turn and run another way.

Claire chased her for a little while before picking her up from behind and cuddling her.

Audrey giggled and giggled.

Claire blew bubbles on her belly, and Audrey laughed even harder.

Addie grinned at the antics of the children. She turned to Douglas. "They'll be all right. I'll get those diapers now."

After washing the diapers, she took the basket outside to the clothesline. She watched the children for a moment and then turned her gaze on her husband.

He had Emmy sitting in his lap. His right leg rested on his left knee forming a sitting area for Emmy. Then he picked her up and put his leg on the ground and held her by her hands, while she stood on his lap facing the other kids.

She bent her knees and bounced on him, looking for all the world like she wanted to join them. Pretty soon, she would be the one out there running with the older children, like Audrey was today.

Addie quickly hung the diapers to dry and then sat

in the chair next to Douglas. She picked up Emmy and cuddled her, kissed her face all over.

Emmy giggled and when Addie stopped, Emmy frowned and started to cry.

Addie kissed her all over again, lifting her gown and blowing against her tummy.

The baby laughed and giggled.

Douglas laughed, too.

Addie stopped and chuckled before blowing against her tummy again and then stopped.

Emmy started to cry each time she stopped, but Addie lifted her by her hands so she was standing, looking out at the other children, just as Douglas had been holding her.

Addie moved to Douglas's lap holding Emmy with both arms around her middle while the baby watched the other children play. "I have to get dinner started."

Douglas looked at his daughter. "Should we let your mama go, Emmy girl? Hmm? Should we let her go?"

The infant gurgled.

Douglas grinned. "Well, you heard her. We're not letting you go. Ever."

Addie laughed and slipped off Douglas's lap, before turning and handing him Emmy. She looked down and he wasn't grinning.

His gaze bored into her. "You heard Emmy."

"She didn't say anything."

"We're not letting you go." He took Emmy with one arm and wrapped the other one around Addie's waist. "We'll never let you go."

She leaned down and kissed him fully on the mouth, just the way he taught her. Addie pulled back and gave him a light peck on the lips. "That's good to knowbecause I don't intend to ever leave…except to go prepare our dinner."

"What are we having?"

"The stew that is simmering on the stove, bread I'll put in the oven when I go in and the last of the canned carrots. I have to add that to my shopping list."

"Sounds good, but no dessert?" His mouth turned down at the corners and he pouted.

She laughed. "In this house? We always have dessert. I baked a peach cobbler this afternoon."

She bent and gave him a quick kiss, turned, picked up the laundry basket and returned to the house. Dropping the basket off on the back porch, she entered the kitchen and checked the stew.

It was bubbling merrily.

She took a wooden spoon and stirred the stew. Then she took the two loaf pans of dough, ready to go, into the oven.

"I guess you'll feed me this time."

At the gravelly voice, Addie dropped the pans on

the counter and spun around and saw Smith leaning against the door jamb leading to the living room with his gun pointed at her. *Why didn't I check the door again when the kids went out back?* "What are you doing here, Joe? People are looking for you."

"Five hundred dollars, dead or alive. I bet most people, you included, would rather see me dead."

She lifted her chin. "I don't mind admitting adopting the kids would be much easier if you were dead."

"Dish me up a bowl of that stew. Right now, if you want to mother those children. I already killed one mother, I don't want to have to kill you, too."

She dished him up a bowl of stew. "I don't believe you meant to kill Edna. You were just drunk and let your temper get the best of you. If you explain that to the sheriff, he might go easy on your sentence."

He waved his gun at her with his left hand, his right hand bandaged.

Addie was afraid the gun would go off by accident.

"Naw, I can't see that happening. The sheriff would as soon kill me as look at me. I'm better off here for now." He sat at the table, keeping his gun on her.

He's not as good with the gun with his left hand. Maybe he won't hit me if he shoots, but what it if goes through the window over the sink and he hits one of the kids? She got him a spoon and then moved back to the stove. *The sooner he's gone the better.* "You can't stay here. Douglas will kill you. Go back to the mine. Maybe you can blend in with the men there."

"Every man knows me and that I'm wanted. Besides, even if I disguised myself, Douglas would know. Do you think he'll let me anywhere near that mine when he discovers I'm the one who set the charges that killed his wife? That was an accident, too. I only meant to kill Josiah. That was all Cassidy wanted. He paid me handsomely for doing it."

"Why didn't you take care of your family?"

"Because I spent it. Lost it at cards and down my gullet in whiskey. That was more important."

"And now? What's important to you now?"

He looked out the window at the children playing in the backyard. "They are. I never should'a done what I done, but I was too drunk to realize what I was doing...or to care. Then. I'm sorry as I can be now. Edna was the light in my life. I always loved her."

I don't want the children to witness their father being killed, too. "Eat. I won't let anything happen to you while you do. I wouldn't let Douglas take you in front of your children no matter what."

Joe put his gun in his holster and dug into the stew.

"When is the last time you ate?"

"Two days ago for a real meal. I stole a steak out

of someone's kitchen while they went to check on their kids. Otherwise, I've been living off other people's scraps. Occasionally I hide by the mines and steal food I know some of the men leave in their saddle bags." He ate more stew and looked behind him at the door. "Get me a piece of paper and a pencil."

Addie did as he asked.

He quickly wrote something on the paper. "Here. Take this to the judge. It'll let you adopt my kids." Joe looked out the window in the back door. "Now, I see Douglas coming. Thank you, Mrs. Latimer, for your kindness." Joe stood and ran out the front door as Douglas came in the back.

"The kids are—Addie you're pale as a ghost. What's the matter?"

"Joe Smith was here. I fed him and he left this for us." She handed Douglas the paper.

November 6, 1871

I give up all rits to my kids. They's to be adopted by Douglas Latimer and Mrs. Latimer.

Joseph William Smith

Addie stared up at Douglas's face. "Is this good enough? Will the judge let us adopt the kids?"

CHAPTER NINE

*D*ouglas held Emmy in his arms. He narrowed his eyes, anger radiating through him. "Why didn't you call for me?" *Another missed opportunity to catch a killer.*

"First, because he had his gun pointed at me." She put her hands on her hips. "Second, because he was just hungry. He left us that paper."

He wasn't letting her off the hook so fast. She should have screamed. "I figured he'd be dead by now. How is he surviving?"

She relaxed, as he wanted her to do.

"Stealing food."

"You should have screamed." His mouth formed a straight line and he clenched his jaw. He directed his ire at Addie now though he knew it shouldn't be.

She pointed at him. Her face was red and her eyes

narrowed. "He would have shot me." Addie opened her arms wide. "Is that what you wish he'd done? You wouldn't have to worry about another child then. You could live with your ghost of Elizabeth. Maybe that painting would keep you warm at night."

"What are you talking about? Ghost of Elizabeth?"

She pointed toward their room. "That portrait of her you put up in our bedroom. The portrait," she pounded on her chest, "that I have to look at every morning and every night. The one of the woman whose memory I can't fight anymore. If it were just me, I'd leave now and let you wallow in your memories."

Douglas realized what he'd done. She was right. He was making her live with his memories of his wife. Elizabeth was gone, and it was time her portrait was too—at least from their bedroom. He handed Emmy to Addie and walked out of the room. He didn't give any explanation but left Addie crying and cuddling the baby.

He heard Emmy start crying, too.

"I'm sorry, baby girl. Mama doesn't mean to upset you."

Walking directly to his and Addie's bedroom, he took down the portrait and carried it to Emmy's room where he placed it facing the wall. Then he walked back out to his wife and daughter.

Douglas went to them and wrapped his arms around them both. "I'm sorry, so very sorry. I was wrong to keep her portrait in our bedroom. My intention is to save it for Emmy, but I'll put it in the barn until she's ready. Please, forgive me, Addie. I don't want you to go." *I could manage without her help, but I don't want to. I need her. Emmy needs her, too. All the kids do. They love her. Do I? Is that the real reason I don't want her to leave?*

---

*A*ddie could have been knocked over with a light breeze. "You're sorry? Really?"

He nodded against the top of her head. "Really. I was very wrong."

She sniffled, stepped back and rocked back and forth with Emmy.

The baby sniffled, too, placed her head on Addie's chest and her thumb in her mouth.

Addie continued to rock her. Emmy was tired, and the crying episode had just made her more so. Addie knew how she felt. She just wanted to curl up into a ball and cry or sleep or both.

"What were you wrong about, exactly?"

"I should never have made you live with that portrait. I guess I wasn't ready to let Elizabeth go."

"And you are now? Why?"

"I am now." He wrapped his arms about her loosely, the baby between them. "I have you and I don't want to lose you. I care for you very much."

"You care for me?" *He cares for me, I'm making headway. He doesn't love me yet, but I hope and believe he will...eventually.*

"Very much." He leaned down and kissed her.

The kiss was gentle, soft. She wrapped one arm around his neck, holding Emmy with the other.

"Forgive me, Addie. Please." He kissed her again.

She pulled back. "I can't stay mad at you when you're kissing me."

He cocked a brow and grinned. "That's the idea. Plus, I like kissing you."

She whispered against his lips, "I have to put our daughter down for her nap."

"I'll come with you."

Addie nodded, stepped out of his arms and headed to Emmy's bedroom. She laid the baby in the crib and then turned back to Douglas. "I wish it was night, and all the children were in bed. I'd let you make love to me."

He pulled her against him. "I wish that, too." Leaning down, he set his lips on hers.

"Addie! Addie!" Claire yelled.

She pulled out of Douglas's arms and ran for the kitchen. "What's the matter? Are you all right?"

Joey ran in carrying a crying Audrey, followed by the rest of the children.

The baby was covered in blood, running down her face from her forehead.

"Here, let me have her. Douglas, ready a basin with warm water, please."

He prepared the water and got a washcloth and towel from the pantry.

The children sat at the kitchen table, their gazes fixed on Audrey.

Addie took the washcloth, dipped it in the water and cleaned Audrey's forehead so she could see the damage.

"What happened?" asked Douglas.

"She was running with the other kids and fell," said Claire. "She must have hit her forehead on a rock because she started screaming and there was blood…"

"It's okay, sweet baby. You'll be fine. Let's just clean this up and see what we have. Shh now. You're okay." Addie took the lye soap she kept on the sink and washed the wound.

Audrey yelled and squirmed nearly out of Addie's arms.

"Douglas, please hold her so she can't wiggle. I'll hold her head so I can wash this and get it clean. Then I have to put some witch hazel on it, and she'll likely scream when I do that."

He took Audrey holding her with one arm around

her chest and the other around her thighs so she couldn't move.

Addie, as gently as possible, cleaned the wound and then applied witch hazel. Then she wrapped the injury with a bandage.

Audrey likely wouldn't keep it on. *How will I keep her from taking it off?* "Claire get me a pair of your socks please." She looked up at Douglas. "It's too late now, and I don't think the wound is too serious, but tomorrow we need to take her to the doctor just to make sure."

"I agree."

Claire ran to her bedroom and returned with a pair of socks, long enough to go to Audrey's shoulder.

Addie took two strips of cotton cloth and tied the socks around Audrey's upper arms so they wouldn't fall off.

"Okay, you can let her go."

Douglas set her on the floor.

She immediately sat and tried to take off the socks over her hands. Then she got mad again and cried.

Addie picked her up and held her, singing and rocking until Audrey wore herself out from crying and fell asleep. Then she and Douglas headed to the babies' room to put her in the crib.

The children started to follow.

Addie turned to them. "She's all right now. Go on outside and play. I promise Audrey will be okay."

After laying Audrey in the crib with Emmy, she and Douglas crept from the room.

In the living room, he took her in his arms and pressed his lips to hers.

"You're a very good mother. Have I told you that, lately?"

Addie smiled. "No, you haven't. You've been quite remiss."

He sighed and waggled his eyebrows. "Tonight I'll make up for today. Be prepared."

She giggled. "I'm always prepared for you." Addie sashayed back to the kitchen and the simmering stew.

---

*R*obert Cassidy sat in his office. When he heard a horse gallop up, he walked to the window and watched as his man, Mack, returned from The Old Glory mine.

The man came into the office.

Robert returned from the window and sat behind his desk. "Did you set the charges?"

"Yes, and I have some news. Josiah left his fortune to his mail-order bride, Adeline Brady. Douglas only owns half."

Robert turned and hit the wall behind him. He

returned his attention to Mack. "How did you find out?"

Mack shrugged. "It's all anyone at the mine could talk about. They wondered if she would start giving orders now. Apparently someone from the judge's office told his wife and it got spread from there."

"And is she giving orders? How could she? She knows nothing about running a mine." He pointed at a chair in front of the desk. "Sit Mack, I don't like looking up at you."

Mack sat in one of the leather chairs. " Douglas still gives the work orders for the day, or at least he gives his foreman, Woodrow Jones, the orders."

Robert stood and paced the small confines of his office "Sounds like she's given over the ownership to Douglas."

Mack crossed a knee over his leg and then put his hat on the opening that was formed. "Wouldn't Douglas own it anyway, because they're married?"

Robert shook his head and hit the desk with his hand. "Even as a married woman, an inheritance gives her the property. I need to get rid of her, too."

"Maybe you could get rid of Douglas and just marry her and take over her half that way. She's got lots of kids to support now. I heard Joe Smith gave his permission for Douglas and Addie to adopt the six Smith kids."

"She wouldn't need to marry. She'd own all of

The Old Glory mine if Douglas is gone. No, she has to go, too."

"Boss, what happens to all those kids if you kill both their parents?"

"I don't know, and I don't care." Robert stared at Mack. He didn't like the soft spot Mack apparently had for the kids. That could be a problem. Perhaps he should arrange for Mack to have an accident. A fatal accident.

The next day, after breakfast, Addie sat with Audrey in the living room. "Joey. Claire. Come here please," she called.

They thundered through the house sounding for all the world like a herd of buffalo, or so she'd been told.

"Yes, Addie," said Claire.

"Yes, ma'am," said Joey. "What do you need?"

"I need the two of you to watch the little ones, including Emmy, while Douglas and I take Audrey to have the doctor look at her head injury."

Claire's eyes widened. "You're really taking her to the doctor?"

Addie tilted her head and furrowed her brows. "Of course. The doctor needs to make sure she doesn't need stitches and that it's not getting infected. Plus she has a fever this morning and he'll tell us how to handle that."

"Wow, we've never been to a doctor…any of us. Even when we was borned, Mama did it at home and one of her women friends helped her. She didn't go to no doctor," said Claire.

"Well, I go to a doctor. And when my baby is born, the doctor will be here to deliver him."

"Him? Do you know it's a boy?" asked Joey.

Addie smiled. "No, but I hope so. And I don't want him to be called *it,* so he's a him."

"We'll watch the kids. I think they should play inside today. It looks like rain." Joey pointed at the window.

Addie followed his arm and gazed out the window. Dark clouds hung over the valley. While she was watching, a snowflake wafted down, followed by another and another. "I think it's snow, not rain. But, in any case we need to wear our heavy coats. Claire, would you dress Audrey appropriately?"

"Yes, ma'am." She bounded up the stairs.

"Emmy is sleeping now but she'll need changing and feeding, in that order, when she wakes up."

Joey rolled his eyes. "I know. I've done it before, remember?"

He sounded exasperated and Addie couldn't blame him. She was entirely too overprotective. He and Claire had been caring for the children for a long time.

Claire returned with Audrey bundled up.

The baby was still hurting, dried tears stained her face and she still sniffled.

Addie grabbed her coat. "Very good."

Douglas came inside and stomped his shoes on the small rug at the entryway. "Let's go before the storm gets too bad to make it back."

Addie looked over at the kids. "If it gets too bad to come back by the time we leave the doctor, we'll stay in town for the night. You two," she pointed at Claire and Joey, "will have to feed the kids and get them to bed. No baths tonight."

"Yay!" The two children shouted at the same time.

Addie rolled her eyes. "Taking a bath is not that bad."

"Easy for you to say. You don't have to bathe after the little kids," said Joey.

Claire nodded.

"Okay, we'll start heating enough water for you both to have clean water for your baths. Will that make you happy?"

"Yay!" shouted Joey. "That'll be great."

Addie kissed each of them on the forehead. "We'll only be as long as we need to be. I promise."

"It's settled then." Addie turned to Douglas. "We're ready now."

Douglas picked up Audrey. "Be careful. It's already starting to get slick outside."

"I'll be careful." She wore a knitted cap and pulled up the collar of her sheepskin coat to protect her neck.

Audrey was dressed in a heavy wool coat, scarf and the little knitted cap they bought on her head, though she still tried to push it and her bandage off. The socks she wore on her hands, now served double duty as mittens.

Douglas wore the same kind of coat as Addie but he wore his Stetson and a wool scarf around his neck. He got them loaded into the buggy and then he got in and took up the reins, slapping them on the horses' butts.

Addie was surprised at the condition of the road. It was completely white, and large flakes were coming down hard and fast. They could be snowed in if they weren't careful.

"We need to hurry at the doctor's if we plan on getting back home sometime this week." Douglas raised his voice to be heard over the clip-clop of the horse's hooves on the snow and the mud underneath.

Even in this terrible time with Audrey hurting, she and Douglas were acting like a loving husband and wife. If only he could love her the way she loved him.

CHAPTER TEN

The trip to the doctor's office wasn't too bad. Addie held on tight to Audrey and gasped when the buggy slid a bit on one of the hairpin curves. Douglas was very adept at keeping the buggy and the horses where they should be.

Arriving at the doctor's office, Douglas pulled up in front of the one-story building with round rocks halfway up the outside wall and whitewashed wood above that.

Douglas set the brake and climbed down. He came around to Addie's side of the conveyance and helped her down and then Audrey fell into his arms. Even though it was snowing he held her so when he turned in a circle she flew.

Addie had to laugh. The snow was coming down like crazy and he played with the child. She knew he was making Audrey happy, and she wasn't scared. A little more of Addie's heart became his.

"Let's go inside and see if Doc is available."

Walking up to the door, Addie knocked once and then entered a small waiting room.

Doctor Collins came out forthwith. "Why, Douglas, good to see you and you brought your beautiful wife."

Addie smiled. "Hi, Doc. We have a little girl here who fell yesterday, banged her forehead and now has a fever."

As if on cue, Audrey pushed at the bandage on her head trying to dislodge it.

"I see you've covered her hands. That's a good thing. Most mothers don't and then they are changing the bandage all the time or leaving it off altogether. Follow me back to the surgery and we'll take care of this little one."

Arriving in the surgery, Addie saw it contained a bed in the middle of the room, a small counter with two cupboards over it and two slat-back wooden chairs on one side of the room.

Doc unwound the dressing and examined the wound. "Whowee! She's got a mighty fine hole in her head. Bled a lot, I bet."

Addie nodded. "It did. I was afraid I wouldn't get it to stop and from the looks of the bandage, I didn't."

"You did fine. This is just a little bit of drainage.

Douglas, hold her, please, so she can't wiggle so much. I need to examine the wound."

Addie handed Audrey to Douglas.

Douglas held her as he had yesterday so she couldn't move.

Doc poked around the injury and dabbed at it with a clean cloth. "It looks good. No infection but if it is to heal right, she'll need a few stitches. I'd like to give her a little chloroform so she doesn't feel it."

"Will it hurt her?" Addie asked.

"No, I'll only give her a very little amount. Just enough to make her sleep for a few minutes."

Addie looked at Douglas.

Douglas turned to the doctor. "Very well. Go ahead."

"Don't worry. By the time I'm finished with the four or five stitches in her forehead, she'll be waking up."

Doc put a couple of drops of the medicine on a cloth and held it over Audrey's nose and mouth.

She stopped wiggling almost immediately.

"Lay her down so we can do this quickly." The doctor pulled a needle with thread in it from a drawer on the cabinet against the wall.

Douglas laid Audrey on the bed that was in the middle of the room.

Doc pointed at the two wooden slat-back chairs

against the wall behind the door. "Why don't you two sit down? Nothing for you to do now."

Addie walked to the chairs.

Her husband guided her with a hand at her waist.

She sat and then almost immediately was up and pacing. "I am just too nervous to sit."

"There, all done. And right on time, too."

Audrey was waking up, her hand went to her forehead and she started crying. "Mama. Mama. Mama."

Oh, my God. She called me Mama. "It's all right baby girl. I'm here." She picked up Audrey and looked at the doctor. "Does she need the bandage on it?"

Doc put his hand on his chin and pulled at a nonexistent beard. "I suppose she can go without it, but you'll have to clean the wound every day, morning and night. Keep her hands covered so she doesn't scratch the stitches open."

"Yes, sir, I will." Addie put a hand to the back of Audrey's head, now resting on Addie's chest. "Is there anything else I need to do?"

"Put some witch hazel on at night after you clean it and bring her back in about ten days to get the stitches removed."

"Will do, Doc," said Douglas. "What do I owe you?"

"Two dollars, which includes the return visit to get the stitches out."

Addie placed a kiss on Audrey's head. "Thanks so much, Doc. I was afraid she might have done more injury to herself than I could see or take care of myself."

"You did well, Addie. Just exactly what you should have done. The injury was very clean, and that's the most important thing. We don't want it to become infected, and I doubt this one will. As to her fever, it's not much of one and will probably be gone by tomorrow."

Douglas held the door for Addie. "By the way, Doc, the snow was coming down hard, when we arrived. Be careful if you have to go out."

"I will. You two be safe getting home."

Douglas nodded. "We will. If it's too bad, we'll get a hotel room. We've already told the children that might happen."

Addie gazed at her husband and then back at Doc. "But we really want to get home if at all possible."

"Of course, you do. You have six more children at home and Emmy is still a baby. I'd want to get home, too."

Douglas urged Addie out the door. "Well thanks, Doc. See you in ten days."

"Goodbye now."

Addie turned and followed Douglas out of the building. As soon as he opened the door to the outside, she was buffeted by wind and snow. She held

Audrey closer, putting down her head she walked out to the buggy.

Douglas brushed the snow from the seat and held Audrey.

Addie climbed up onto the seat and took Audrey in her arms.

He hurried around the surrey, climbed in and slapped the reins.

The horses began to walk.

He slapped the lines again.

The horses trotted up the incline to the first turn onto Douglas's road.

He slowed them to a walk. His tire tracks were already covered with fresh snow.

The storm swirled around them and Addie hugged the baby tight in her arms.

Douglas negotiated the second switchback and only slid a little. The last hairpin curve was coming up.

As the horses took the turn, the buggy slid sideways, and the back wheel on Addie's side slipped off the road.

Addie screamed, her heart thumping in her chest so hard she was sure the sound could be heard.

Douglas slapped the reins on the horses' backs. They sped up, pulled the conveyance into the middle of the road and kept going all the way home.

Upon arriving, he stopped by the front door. He

got down and went around helping Addie to the ground by holding Audrey.

When she was safely down, she took Audrey and started toward the house.

"I'll be in after I take care of the horses."

"Bring a load of wood off the back porch when you come, please. I think we'll need it."

He nodded and climbed back into the buggy taking it toward the barn.

Addie knocked until Joey let her in. She entered the blessed warmth of the house. She stopped by the door and undressed Audrey from her coat and hat.

"Okay, baby girl, go play with your brothers and sisters."

Audrey ran into the living room where the children were playing.

In the kitchen, Claire was preparing chili for lunch.

"Mmm something smells good."

Claire looked up. "It was one of my mother's recipes." She held up a recipe card. "How is Audrey?"

"She's fine. Doc put in five stitches, so she'll have a little scar, that's all. Do you want cornbread to go with the chili?"

"Oh, yes, that would be great."

"I'll be right back." Addie walked toward the living room and hung up Audrey's garments in the coat closet off the hallway. She removed hers as well.

She returned to the kitchen and mixed the cornbread and put the pan in the hot oven. "The bread will be ready in about a half-hour. What about the chili?"

Claire gave the pot of chili a couple of stirs to keep it from burning on the bottom. "It's ready now but I'll keep it simmering until it's time to eat."

Douglas walked in from outside and stomped his boots. "Something smells wonderful. What do you have cooking, Claire?"

She smiled and blushed. "Chili from my mother's recipe."

"I do remember that Edna was a good cook before she got sick."

Claire's face fell a little but then she looked up with a smile. "Yes, she was. A very good cook and I have her recipe box. It's got recipes for lots of different things."

Addie walked to Claire and put an arm around her shoulders. "Well, maybe we should start looking through that and making our weekly grocery shopping for those recipes we want to make. What do you think?"

Claire grinned from ear to ear. "I think Mama would've liked that a lot. Thank you."

"Don't thank me. It's the least we can do to preserve her memory."

The girl turned and hugged her.

Addie put her hands on Claire's back and hugged her.

She hoped she could develop a relationship with Claire and maybe she was. Was she being a good mother? Her fear that she wasn't kept her awake some nights. Maybe this hug was the start of a connection with this child. She would take them one at a time, but Joey would be the hardest. Could he learn to love Addie too?

Douglas had come in from outside and saw his wife and Claire hug. He smiled as he carried an armload of firewood into the living room.

Joey had a blaze going in the fireplace, and Douglas was grateful for the warmth after being outside. He feared the blaze was too big though. "Joey let's let the fire die down a bit before we add more wood. It's a little hot in here."

Joey sat on the sofa with Audrey looking at a children's book they'd brought from the Smith home. "Sure. I know what you mean."

Emmy cried from her room.

"Sounds like someone is awake," said Douglas. "I'll get her. You can keep an eye on Audrey. She wants to scratch her stitches but the doctor wants them in for ten days, so except for baths, she has to wear the socks on her arms."

"Okay. I'll watch her."

Douglas hurried to his daughter's room.

Her cries were getting louder and louder.

"What's the matter, little girl? Are you wet? I bet you are." He removed her soaked dress and then her soaker and her diaper. He should have expected it but he didn't and wasn't prepared for the stench that hit his nose. "Oh, my goodness. What has Mama been feeding you? That's okay, we'll just get you cleaned up and dry."

He put the dirty diaper in the bucket and quickly covered it. Then he washed her with soap and water before rinsing her with a clean washcloth. He diapered her in a heavy diaper and clean soaker, before pulling a clean dress over her head and put her arms through the appropriate openings. Whoever said men couldn't take care of babies had obviously never met a father without a wife for any length of time.

Douglas picked up his daughter and took her to the kitchen.

"Hi, Mama," he said as he entered the room.

Addie turned from the sink where she was doing the pots and pans they'd used to make lunch and her face lit up. "Well, hello there, sweetheart. Did you just get up? You smell all fresh and clean, so Daddy must have changed you. Is that right, Daddy?"

"It is. She had messed her pants, and I just put the diaper in the bucket, so beware."

Addie tilted her head and smiled. "Thanks for the warning. There is a second, smaller pail up there for messy diapers."

Douglas shrugged. "I guess I must have missed it."

"It doesn't matter. I should have told you about the pail but I forgot. It's something new I added to the babies' room. You got her all clean and dry and that's all that matters. I bet she's hungry. If you give her a bottle, I'll scramble an egg for her."

"Okay."

Addie fixed Emmy's bottle before handing it to him. She'd started supplementing the formula with bits of egg and mashed potatoes. He knew seven children demanded her being available for them, too.

She got out the smallest skillet they had which was only big enough to fry two eggs at a time and cracked an egg into it. She quickly scrambled the egg and put it in a bowl to cool.

Douglas was still amazed at how well Addie cared for the children. Two weeks ago he'd taken Joe Smith's note to the judge along with other paperwork needed for the adoption. He hadn't told Addie yet because he was waiting to hear from Judge Baker. This weather would make that news even longer in coming. He sighed. Unfortunately he couldn't do anything about the weather.

, check on the mine, too. Instead of walking, he'd use the sleigh to get around. It was large enough he could take the whole family and by going to the mine first, he'd be able to tell if the road was too slick for the sleigh.

He snapped his fingers. That's what they needed —a family outing. They could go to the top of Virginia Gulch and have a frozen picnic. No, it would be too cold for that, especially for the babies. But getting out in the snow and fresh air would be good for them all.

They would go to the mercantile and get candy for everyone. Joyce usually had hot chocolate on the pot-bellied stove when the weather was like this. Douglas smiled. That was a perfect idea, but he would go to the mine and see how the roads were and how the sleigh acted on the ice that was surely underneath.

That night Addie got ready for bed. All the children were already in their beds, hopefully fast asleep by now.

She let down her hair and watched in the mirror of her dressing table, a present from Douglas when he got the cribs. He smiled, his gaze trapping hers in the mirror.

Placing her brush on the table, she turned to face him. Her dressing gown had fallen open, but she didn't bother with it. "You seem rather chipper tonight."

"I'm lying in bed, watching my beautiful wife undress to join me here. What is there not to be happy about?"

"Okay, mister. You've got something on your mind. I see it in your eyes. They have that mischievous twinkle."

He feigned outrage and placed a hand on his chest and one on his forehead as he'd seen actors and actresses do on stage. "Who, me? Oh, woe is me. My wife doesn't trust me."

Addie giggled and dropped her dressing gown over a chair. She climbed under the covers and scooted close to him, to his warmth. Shivering, she cuddled and put a leg over his, gathering all the heat she could. "It's cold out there. I wonder why Josiah didn't put a fireplace in this room."

Douglas wrapped an arm around her shoulders. "Probably because he didn't spend much time here at the house and often, when he did, he slept on the living room sofa. That's why it's so long. He was a tall man, a couple of inches taller than me."

She settled against him, a hand on his chest. "I

kind of wish I'd gotten to know Josiah and been able to tell him how much he's meant to the both of us. I wouldn't be married to you, if not for him. I wouldn't own half The Old Glory mine or this house, if not for him. In a strange way, I think maybe he's kind of responsible for us having the Smith children."

He rubbed her back. "He was a good man. You would have liked him, probably loved him. He was just that kind of man."

She ran her fingers through the sprinkling of hair on his chest. "I can tell you loved him like a brother. His death, and Elizabeth's, would have been hard to accept."

Douglas squeezed her shoulders and then returned to rubbing her back. "I had Emmy to care for. She was my savior. She kept me from falling into a deep depression."

She looked up at him.

He stared at the ceiling with his other arm behind his head.

She kissed his chest. "What about when I came? You could have wallowed in your grief then and not worried about Emmy, knowing I would care for her. But you didn't. You warned me of certain things, but you also made sure to be here for us."

"I want to be a good husband to you. That's all. A good husband and father. I love these kids…all of them and I care for you deeply."

"I care for you, too."

He turned her onto her back and leaned over her, covering her body with his. "I want you to more than care for me. I hope you will someday." He dropped his head and took her lips with his while his hand explored her body.

She wrapped her arms around him and wondered if she could love him enough for the both of them.

CHAPTER ELEVEN

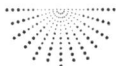

The next morning, the sun shone brightly. The snow covered everything as far as the eye could see and sparkled like it was embedded with diamonds.

Breakfast was done.

Joey washed the dishes.

Claire dried them and put them away.

The kids started doing this without her asking. She was so proud of the children.

"Now that I have you all together, I'm hitching up the sleigh and going to town. Anyone interested in going for a ride?" Douglas stood with his arms crossed over his chest.

"Oh, yes!" shouted Claire.

"Me! Me! Me!" yelled Joey.

Addie laughed. "I believe we'd all like to go. If the roads are all right."

Douglas smiled. "I went to the mine yesterday and they were good. We shouldn't have any trouble and I'll make sure the horses' only walk. In any case, that's what I wanted to hear. I'll get the sleigh ready and you can get everyone ready to go. Dress very warm and bring blankets to cover your laps."

The kids ran out of the kitchen.

Addie walked over to her husband and wrapped her arms around his waist. "What is the occasion? First, last night in bed, and now this. If I didn't know better, I'd say you were wooing me."

"We know how far that would get me if I was."

"Farther than you might think." She unwrapped her arms and turned to leave.

He grabbed her arm and pulled her back to him. Douglas stared down, tucked a strand of hair behind her ear and then kissed her.

His kiss was not gentle, but possessive.

Douglas pulled back. "Never doubt that I want you. Probably more than I should, but I can't seem to help myself where you are concerned." He gave her a quick peck and then grabbed his coat from a peg on the wall and walked out the door.

Addie stood there for a moment with two fingers on her lips. *He can't help himself where I'm concerned. Does that mean he loves me and doesn't want to?* She smiled.

She didn't have time to contemplate the meaning behind his words. The children needed to dress for the ride. Babies to change diapers on and put in their coats and blankets. She'd bought knitted hats for the children including the babies and now she was glad she did.

By the time all the children were in their winter clothes and coats, Douglas pulled the sleigh up to the kitchen door.

He came in and took Audrey.

Addie carried Emmy.

The older children took the hands of the younger ones and everyone filed out of the house into the sleigh.

Addie looked at him and jutted her head toward the house. "I have three blankets on the kitchen table, but we all had our hands full with little children. Would you give Audrey to Joey and grab those blankets, please?"

"Certainly." He waited for Joey to get settled in the seat and then gave him his baby sister to hold.

Joey, Audrey and Larry sat in the rear seat.

Claire, Sara and Rami sat in the middle seat.

Addie sat in the front, holding Emmy.

The baby squealed and kicked, waving her arms, thoroughly happy to be out in the cold.

Douglas came out with the blankets and handed one to Joey, one to Claire and put one on the seat between him and Addie, before climbing into the sleigh.

"Everyone ready to go?" he shouted to the children behind him.

He received a resounding chorus of yeses and nary a single negative response.

Once he was seated, Addie spread the blanket so it covered his lap and hers. She was glad of the extra warmth. The morning might be beautiful but it was also freezing. She was colder than she ever remembered being. Her father was not a person who liked this kind of weather, so he made sure to be in those cold locations anytime but winter. The winter months she'd spent in Arizona Territory or in California. Plenty of saloons to ply his trade in both of those areas.

Gliding across the snow, Douglas took one of the hairpin curves a little fast causing the sleigh to slide around. Addie screamed as did the children.

He laughed. "I'm sorry. I couldn't resist." He looked behind him. "Everyone okay back there."

"We're fine," grumbled Joey.

The sleigh made quick work of the trip to town, to the courthouse for the first stop. Douglas ran in and, when he came out, he had a big smile on his face. He turned toward the children in the back of the sleigh. "I have some good news. At least I hope it's good news. Your father gave us permission to adopt all of you, and I gave that paper to the judge. He has agreed and said the paperwork I've already filed, plus the letter from Joe, is all I needed. You all are officially Latimers now. How do you feel about that?"

Most of the children yelled and laughed.

Addie grinned, her heart near to bursting.

"Can we call you Mama and Daddy now?" asked Claire.

Addie smiled. "You sure can. I would be very happy if you did. I love you like you're my own children, and now you are."

The only quiet person was Joey.

Addie tilted her head toward him and mouthed to Douglas, "Talk to him."

Douglas turned so he was facing Joey. "What about you, Joey? Are you happy? Or would you rather not change what you call us? You can do either, and it's okay."

Joey looked away. "I don't know what I want. I need to think about it."

Addie felt sad for Joey. He loved his father and mother very much, which is not to say the other children didn't but as the oldest, he seemed to feel their absence more.

Douglas continued to look at the boy. "Take all the time you need, son. We are here for you and we're not going anywhere." He turned back facing the front and dropped the reins on the horses' rears and got them moving again. Next stop was the mercantile.

Everyone got out and went inside. The proprietress, Joyce Davis, had a pot of hot chocolate on the potbellied stove, along with a coffee pot.

"Well, good morning, Latimers. How are you all this fine morning? I bet you children would like some hot chocolate. Am I right?"

"Oh, yes, ma'am," said Claire.

All the children gathered 'round, and Joyce poured them cups of the sweet, hot liquid.

Joyce turned to Addie as a tall young man approached. "Addie, this is my oldest son, Seth. He'll help you out with the groceries from now on."

Douglas held Audrey and Addie held Emmy, so the kids could fully enjoy the hot drink.

Claire shared a few sips of her drink with Audrey, though she was careful because the liquid was quite hot.

"We also need several candy sticks, two pounds of fudge…do you have any penuche?" asked Addie.

"I make that myself and just finished a batch this morning."

"Then I'd like two pounds of penuche, too."

"You got it." Joyce took out her scale and weighed the candy. "How many candy sticks?"

"We'll take two of each flavor with us and the

kids each get one now." Addie looked up at Douglas. "As long as we have the sleigh can we do a bit of shopping while we're here?"

"Of course. That makes the most sense."

Addie walked through the store with a burlap bag picking up canned vegetables and fruit, and yeast. She also ordered one-hundred pounds of flour and seventy-five of sugar, twenty-five pounds of cornmeal and ten pounds of oats.

"That should do it for now. It will get us through for another week of meals, maybe more."

The bell above the door sounded as someone entered.

"Well, well, well. If it isn't the Latimers and the Smith brats."

Robert Cassidy sneered at the children who gathered around Addie.

"Joey, would you take your baby sister, please?" Douglas gave Audrey to her brother.

"Why don't you leave, Cassidy?" Douglas didn't raise his voice but his hands were fisted at his sides. "No one wants you here, probably including Joyce."

"Ah, but I have shopping to do." He picked up a can off the shelf nearest him. "See?" He held up the can.

Douglas narrowed his eyes. "Pay for your peas and get out."

"I don't believe I shall. This is much too entertaining, seeing you all here. You wouldn't want to hit me in front of the children, now would you?"

Douglas looked at Addie.

She shrugged.

Apparently that was all Douglas needed. He punched Cassidy with a right to the jaw.

Addie heard Joey talking to Audrey. "That's our new dad. He won't let anything bad happen to us."

She couldn't have been more pleased. Joey was beginning to accept Douglas as his father.

Cassidy jabbed at Douglas.

He blocked the blow and gave him one to his already broken nose.

Addie flinched when she heard the cartilage in Cassidy's nose break and saw blood flow down his face.

"You batherd. You broke my nose, again." He took a handkerchief from his inside coat pocket and put it over his nose.

"If you want more, keep insulting my children. They are all my children, legally adopted. If you have something to say to me, do it at the mine."

Cassidy abruptly left holding his nose.

Douglas turned to Addie. "I'm sorry you had to witness his boorish behavior again."

She shook her head. "Nothing to be sorry about. If I hadn't been holding Emmy, I'd have taken a shot at him myself."

Douglas grinned and packed up everything into a couple of boxes. The flour, sugar and cornmeal were in prepackaged bags.

"Joey, would you help me carry this out to the sleigh, please?"

The boy shrugged and picked up one of the boxes.

Douglas picked up the other.

Seth carried the flour.

Douglas came back in and got the sugar and cornmeal.

Addie made sure each child had a candy stick, except Emmy.

They all went out and boarded the sleigh.

Once everyone was aboard, Douglas looked back and then started the horses back home.

By the time they arrived, the children were cold.

Addie turned to Joey. "Would you build a fire when we get inside, please? You're so good at it."

He shrugged. "I thought Douglas said I built it too big."

"That was for that particular day. Today we need a big fire, don't you think?"

Joey lifted one shoulder and nodded. "Yes, I guess so. All the little kids are shivering and ready to go inside."

Addie nodded. "Yes, they are. Once they get their coats off they'll really be cold, so a roaring fire is just what we'll need."

"I can do that." He turned to Claire. "Would you help the kids off with their coats, while I make the fire?"

She nodded. "I will."

Douglas stopped the sleigh in the back by the kitchen. He set the brake and got out ran to the door, unlocked it and ran back to help Addie and Claire down to the ground without slipping on the iron steps.

Addie set Emmy on the floor of the sleigh while Douglas helped her down. Then she picked the baby back up and cuddled her. "Are you cold, Emmy? I'll warm you up once we get inside."

She hurried into the kitchen.

Joey ran to the living room and started the fire.

All the kids, and Addie, too, followed him.

When the fire warmed up the room a bit, the children began shedding their coats.

Addie unwrapped Emmy and took off her coat, but she left her in the little knitted pants, sweater and hat. The hat would do a lot to keep her warm. She read somewhere that a person would stay warmer if he wore a hat.

"Claire, would you hold Emmy while I take care of the blankets?"

"Sure. The kid's coats are on the floor where they put them. I was about to hang them up."

. . .

*A*ddie smiled. "I'll do that. She gathered the blankets and folded them placing them in the bottom of the hall closet. Then she picked up the coats where the children left them and hung them in the closet.

Douglas entered the kitchen and stomped his feet to get off the snow.

She looked up when he came in. "You don't have to worry about taking off your boots. It's too cold right now to go shoeless."

"Are the kids all in the living room?"

"Yes, why?"

"Just this." He wrapped his arms around her waist and drew her flush with his body. Then he traced her hair as it lay against her face. "You are so very beautiful. Have I told you how lucky I am that you agreed to marry me?"

She linked her arms behind his neck. "No, I don't believe you ever have."

"That is a mistake on my part. I'm the luckiest man alive." He took her lips and melded his to hers. He pressed against her closed mouth and met her tongue when she opened, but there was nothing playful about this kiss. She took advantage of his ardor and added her own to his. Putting all of her love for him into the kiss.

She pulled back and rested her forehead on his chest just below his chin. "Douglas."

He kissed the top of her head. "I know, but I won't forget our little interlude and will continue it tonight in private."

She looked up at him and grinned. "Yes, you will, because I won't let you forget, either."

Claire walked into the kitchen. "Are you two done? My goodness, you can't keep your hands off of each other."

Addie laughed. "You're just nine. You'll understand better in about seven years."

Douglas turned toward the living room. "I think I'll join the kids and leave you ladies to it."

Once he'd left, Claire put her arms behind her back. "I came to tell you that tomorrow is Joey's birthday, and I think I'd like to make him a cake. Would you help me?"

"You bet. Do you know what his favorite kind is?"

"Chocolate with chocolate frosting."

"Sounds good. We have all the ingredients for that. Maybe it will make him a little happier."

Claire clasped her hands in front of her and stared at the floor while she rocked back and forth. "He just don't want us to forget our father and mother. It don't matter that father's a murderer and killed our mother. He wants us to remember him." She put her hands on her hips. "I'll remember Mama, but all I remember of Father is he was a drunk that let us go hungry and then killed our mama."

Addie was taken aback at the anger in Claire's voice. She was definitely angry at her father *and* her brother, but she was trying hard to understand Joey. "I think once he gets used to the idea of us being his parents now and we only want what's best for all of you, he'll calm down."

Claire tilted her head and furrowed her brows. "What are siblings? I've heard you say that before."

Addie put an arm around the girl's shoulders. "They're your brothers and sisters. That's another word for them, siblings."

Claire thought for a moment and then nodded. "I think that's a good word. Siblings. I'll remember that." She looked up at Addie. "Can I start a new book tonight? Mama taught us to read and write."

"Is this one for you to read to your siblings or just one to read yourself, for enjoyment?"

"Just for me to read. I saw one called *Pride and Prejudice* on the bookshelf. I read a bit of it already and think it's a romance." Claire turned bright red. "I thought I might like it for a change."

"You can certainly read that one if you want. Josiah had lots of books. A couple more by Jane Austen are on the bookshelves. Also you'll find one called *Jane Eyre* by Charlotte Bronte. My favorite, however, is *Little Women* by Louisa May Alcott."

"Maybe I'll try that one."

"When you finish it, you'll have to let me know how you liked it and maybe we can compare our favorite parts."

Claire wrapped her arms around Addie's waist. "I'm glad you're my mama now."

Addie hugged her back. "I'm glad, too. Shall we get started on that cake?"

Claire nodded. "I'll get the bowl."

Addie watched the girl collect the ingredients for the cake. Claire had grown up so much since her mother died. She was so proud of her and of Joey, too. They'd taken responsibility for the younger kids, cared for them, hugged them when they hurt themselves, and dished up their plates at meals…whatever the children needed, Claire and Joey took care of it.

Douglas entered the kitchen from the living room. "Guess who I ran into, just passing by before I came in."

Addie could tell by the sound of his voice he was not happy. "I have no idea."

"Robert Cassidy. He said he was coming to check on you. Make sure you were safe and see if you needed anything. Why would he think I couldn't provide for you, especially after that episode at the mercantile?"

She went about measuring flour and sugar for the cake. "I haven't any idea."

Claire was creaming the eggs, butter and vanilla together.

"Did you talk to him on your own?"

She saw Claire quietly leave the kitchen. *Smart girl.* Addie turned to face him and put her hands on her hips. "No. You've been with me whenever I saw him. What's gotten into you?"

"Elizabeth was having or had an affair with Cassidy. I think she was meeting him at the mine and Josiah saw her. I don't believe for a minute she was having an affair with Josiah. He wouldn't do that to me. But I think he confronted her about it."

"And you're saying she did? Therefore you think I would?"

"Yes, why else would Cassidy come by to check on you?"

Addie stared at her husband, her stomach in knots and her hands in fists. "Perhaps he wants you to think exactly what you're thinking. The next thing you'll say is this baby I carry isn't yours. Is that what you're thinking? Well, you are wrong on all counts and I won't stand here and be accused of something I haven't done."

She turned to leave.

He grabbed her arm and pulled her to him. "Don't you walk away from me."

Addie shook off his hand and put distance between them, walking to the stove, before turning back toward him, eyes narrowed and her mouth turned down. "Then don't accuse me of things that aren't true. I would never, ever cheat on you. My marriage vows are sacred to me, but they must not be to you, if you think it's so easy to forget them."

Douglas took a deep breath and ran a hand behind his neck. "I'm sorry. I should never have compared you to Elizabeth or suggested you might forget your wedding vows. It's just when Cassidy—"

She held up a hand, palm out. "It doesn't matter what Cassidy does or doesn't do. The situation comes down to whether you trust me or not, and obviously you do not. Why don't you talk to me again when you've decided to trust me and not before?" She turned and left the room. She'd come back when he was gone from the kitchen to finish Joey's cake. She would not let Douglas ruin the celebration of the boy's eleventh birthday.

Addie went back into the kitchen when she was sure Douglas was with the children.

Claire joined her.

"Shall we finish that cake for Joey? I thought maybe we could celebrate tonight, would that be okay with you?"

The girl nodded and then bit her lip. "Are you and

Douglas going to get rid of us if you get unmarried?"

Addie knelt in front of the girl. "Douglas and I are not getting unmarried for any reason…ever. Grownups fight sometimes and only with words. Douglas would never hit me. You don't have to worry about either of us leaving you. Understand? We love you and you've just become a Latimer, why would we do that if we were about to divorce?"

Clair shrugged. "I don't know. I just know when Mama and Father used to fight, he always hit her."

"That will never happen in this house," said Douglas from the doorway leading to the living room. "Trust us on this. You will always be safe here and Addie and I love you all very much."

Addie didn't look at him. "Now, Claire and I must finish this cake if we are to have it tonight."

"Of course." He turned and left the way he came.

Taking a deep breath, Addie stood. "Shall we finish this cake and then get that roast in the oven for dinner?"

Claire smiled. "Yes, Mama."

Every time she heard one of the children call her mama, Addie's heart was just a little happier.

After dinner was done and everyone had gotten their fill, Addie stood and went to the counter returning with the chocolate cake.

As she walked she sang.
For he's a jolly good fellow
For he's a jolly good fellow
For he's a jolly good fellow
That nobody can deny

Addie set the cake in the middle of the table. "We hope you have a very happy birthday tomorrow and hope you don't mind if we celebrate a little early."

Joey grinned from ear to ear. "Ain't never celebrated my birthday before." He looked at Douglas and then Addie. "Thanks."

"You're welcome. What do you say we cut this and have some birthday cake for our dessert, assuming, of course, that you want to share it with us."

"Huh? Oh, yes. Definitely," said Joey.

Addie got plates, forks and a large cake knife. She cut slices for all the kids, with Joey and Douglas getting the largest pieces. When she handed Joey his, she smiled at him. "In honor of your birthday, if you," she looked around the table. "And only you, want to have the leftover cake for breakfast on your actual birthday, you may."

"Really? I'd like that." He shoveled another bite of the chocolate treat into his mouth.

Addie lifted an eyebrow and lowered her chin. "Just because it's your birthday doesn't mean you and talk with your mouth full."

The boy turned red and then swallowed before talking again. "Yes, ma'am." He may have been chastised a bit, but that didn't remove the smile from his face.

She was thrilled that he enjoyed it so much.

"You must thank your sister for telling me it was your birthday coming up and thank her for the cake since she made most of it."

Claire smiled down at her plate, blushing.

Joey looked over at his sister, eyes wide. "Really? Thanks, Claire."

She looked up and grinned. "You're welcome."

Like the proud mama she was, Addie smiled at her family. Now, all she had to do to make everything perfect was for Douglas to love her, not just care deeply, but love her totally. Could that ever happen?

CHAPTER TWELVE

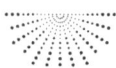

For two weeks Addie barely spoke to Douglas, and then only in front of the children and only to answer a question or to ask one. She wore her nightgown to bed and made sure she stayed on her side.

Somehow or another, she always seemed to wake up in Douglas's arms just as she'd done this morning. She tried to dislodge herself from his grasp.

"I see you're awake."

"Yes, now let me go."

"I'll never let you go, Addie. Never."

"What are we doing, Douglas? You don't love me. I think you only stay for the children, which is admirable, but it's not enough." Despite her promise to herself, she broke down into tears.

"Shh." He pulled her closer. "I've discovered

many things about our marriage, about you and, most of all, about me. I'm an ass. I know that now. I should never have accused you of having an affair with Cassidy. Sometimes, when you love someone, jealousy, that green-eyed monster, gets the better of you."

She stopped struggling, her heart lighter than it was in a long time. "Love? You…you love me?"

He chuckled. "Yes, I love you, more than I ever could have imagined possible."

"But I thought—"

He turned to his side, keeping his arm around her. "I know, and I'm sorry I didn't say it to you sooner, but I just realized it myself. I know that I've loved you for a long time…maybe since I first saw you. You see I really hadn't gone down there planning on marrying you. I thought it might be possible but until I saw you, saw how you took to Emmy right away, I'd planned on telling you about Josiah's death, and giving you enough money to go back to wherever you wanted to go."

I can't believe he loves me. My dreams are coming true and I want to leap for joy. She ran a hand up his arm and rested it on his chest over his heart. "Of course, then you would have had to find me when you found Josiah's will."

"That's true, but I didn't know that then. Addie? Can you find it in your heart to love me, too?"

He sounded so scared.

She couldn't leave him hanging any longer. "But I do love you and have nearly forever. Every time I saw you with Emmy, I fell a little more in love with you. I could see you loved her so much, and you were so gentle with her."

"Why didn't you tell me?"

She moved so she was lying on top of him and wrapped her arms around his neck. "Because you were so sure you'd never love me, I didn't want you to feel guilty for not loving me back...and, selfishly I didn't want to be the only one in this relationship in love." She kissed him slowly, thoroughly. "I'll never give my heart to anyone else. It's yours...forever."

A pounding on their bedroom door sounded, ending their conversation.

"Who is it?" said Douglas loudly.

"Claire. Please, I need your help."

Douglas stood and put on his pants.

Addie donned her robe. It was still dark outside and couldn't have been much past four o'clock. As she passed by the bureau, she looked at the clock—four-fifteen.

Douglas reached the door first. "What is it, Claire? What's wrong?"

She wrung her hands and then pointed toward the front door. "Joey's gone. I think he went to the mine to look for Father. He's been missing him, even though he killed Mama. I'll never forgive him for that, but Joey is different."

Douglas grabbed his shirt. "I'll get him. What makes him think Joe is at Old Glory mine?"

Claire clasped her hands in front of her. "He heard Father when he came to the house and made Addie feed him. Then he found this note under the kitchen door when he went out to milk the cow."

Addie saw how much she was shaking. She went to her and put her arms around Claire's shoulders. "Douglas will find him. Don't worry. Let me see the note."

Claire handed the message to Addie. "I can't help worrying. Joey has never accepted that Father is a bad man now. He remembers when we were small and Father would come home and play with us, when we had plenty to eat and he treated Mama so nice. But he changed and became an evil man."

Addie rubbed Claire's back absentmindedly while she read the note. "Liquor has that effect on people sometimes." Addie read the note. "Listen to this."

Joey. I need you, son. Meet me at the entrance to The Old Glory mine at five in the morning. Please, son. Dad

Douglas sat on the bed and put on his boots. "Claire, how long do you think Joey's been gone?"

The girl shook her head. "I don't know. He was

gone when I went to get him to do our morning chores just now."

Addie gazed over at Douglas. "Well, since he probably found the message when he went out to do the milking, he's only been gone less than an hour. Unless he took a horse, it'll take him at least an hour to walk to the mine. You'd better hurry. Your first shift is about to start and I don't want Joey going down into the mine looking for his father."

"Oh, yes, please hurry, Papa," said Claire.

Douglas stopped midway through pulling on his boot. "Papa?"

Claire looked at her feet and swayed back and forth. "I hope you don't mind."

He walked over to her, knelt and took her in his arms. "Nothing could make me happier. Thank you, little gir—Claire. I can't call you a little girl anymore. You're growing up right before our eyes."

She threw her arms around his neck and hugged him tightly. "Thank you for being my papa and adopting all of us."

"You're very welcome. It was my—" He looked up at Addie. "Our pleasure."

Addie nodded and felt tears in her eyes. "As much as I would like this moment to continue, you have to get Joey."

He pulled on his second boot. "I'll see you in a little while."

Douglas ran out of the bedroom.

A couple of minutes later, Addie heard the kitchen door slam shut. "Claire, you'll have to milk the cow and I'll gather the eggs. I don't know how to milk or I'd do it. The babies are still asleep, let's hope they stay that way."

The child ran out of the room and down the stairs.

Again, Addie heard the door slam.

She hurried and dressed. Since the snow two weeks ago, the weather had been unseasonably warm, but it was still quite cold in the mornings before the sun rose. She dressed in a dark blue wool dress, plain except for white collar and cuffs. Then she put on her gun, her boots with the knife in them and hurried down the stairs.

Addie went out to gather the eggs. She grabbed a lantern and lit it, then picked up the egg basket.

"I'm so glad to see that you haven't forgotten your roots before you got rich."

She screamed and backed up, nearly falling off the porch. Turning quickly, she saw Robert Cassidy sitting on the porch railing, in the dark. "Robert, what are you doing here?"

"Why, waiting for you, my dear. I knew you'd be the one to come out to do the chores if I got the boy out of the way. I knew Douglas would have to go after him, leaving you to do the boys chores."

Addie's heart pounded in her chest and her mind

spun trying to find a way to get to her gun. Douglas and Joey were in danger. She had to help them. "Why do you care who does the chores?"

Cassidy gave a bark of laughter. "I don't. What I do care about is getting you alone." He pulled his pistol and pointed it. "Now you're coming with me. I need you to sign over your interest in The Old Glory mine."

Addie laughed until tears ran down her face, not from laughter but from fear, but she couldn't let him know. "You've outmaneuvered yourself. I don't own any part of The Old Glory. I signed over my interest in the mine to Douglas almost immediately."

Cassidy cursed loudly. "Why would you do that?"

"Because I know nothing about mining, and the mine really is Douglas's baby."

"Well, I guess that doesn't really matter. I've got charges set to collapse the mine and kill anyone inside."

Addie's heart pounded in her chest. "You lie."

"Look at me, Addie. Am I lying?"

She saw in his eyes he was telling the truth. The smile on his face told her he was happy about it, too. Addie moved farther away from him. "What do you expect to happen if you kill Douglas? Do you expect to get me to sign over the mine then? I can't. If Douglas dies, the mine ownership goes into a trust for the children and me. The trustee is Judge Baker.

You'll have to talk to him about selling you the mine." She hoped her bluff would make him leave so she could get to the mine and warn Douglas.

He cursed again, louder this time.

"You can curse all you want, but you'll never get your hands on The Old Glory mine. You might as well leave here before Douglas returns. And he will be back. Joe Smith told us about the charges Mack set in the mine. Joe rendered them useless. It was his way of saying thank you to us for adopting his children."

As if on cue, Addie heard a horse gallop up. Then she lowered her chin. "You better get out of here while the getting is good, Robert. You won't get another chance once Douglas sees you."

Cassidy looked from her to the barn door and then back at her. He holstered his pistol and jumped off the porch into the dark.

She heard him run and then a horse gallop away. Addie looked toward the barn where Joey opened the large doors.

Douglas rode in and slid from the saddle.

Addie rushed to him and threw her arms around him. "Douglas, Cassidy was here. He's the one who left the note for Joey. He admitted he has the mine rigged to blow up just like with Josiah."

Hugging her close, he kissed the top of her head. "It's okay. We took care of the dynamite he'd set in the mine."

Joey stood behind them. "My dad didn't leave me the note?"

Addie turned toward the boy. "I'm sorry, son. It wasn't."

The child's eyes filled with tears but he didn't cry. "If you want, I'll gather the eggs."

She knew he needed some time alone. "I'd appreciate that very much. I'll get breakfast started."

Douglas turned to Joey. "I'll be using Star again, but would you give him a flake of hay for me?"

Joey nodded. "I'll take care of him. Don't worry."

Douglas walked over to the boy. "I'm not worried. I know you are very capable and I trust you."

The boy gazed up at him. "You trust me even after taking off this morning?"

"Yes, I do. I understand a boy needs his father. I hope, someday you'll let me be that man."

Joey looked at his feet and then up at Douglas. With a cry, he ran to Douglas and wrapped his arms around his waist. "I want you to be my father." He gazed up at the tall man. "Please."

"Nothing would make me happier." He hugged the boy.

Tears filled Addie's eyes. She blinked them away but they rolled down her cheeks anyway.

"Where are you going?" Addie was afraid she knew and felt fear like she never had before.

"I'm confronting Cassidy and taking him to the sheriff."

Addie's breath caught in her throat and her hands shook. "You can't go. He'll be ready for you. He'll kill you."

He walked over and squeezed her to him, resting his head on top of hers. "I have to go, you know that. I can't let him get away with Josiah and Elizabeth's murders, as well as planning mine."

Joe Smith walked out of the shadows in the back of the barn. "Why don't you take me with you? I owe you for taking in my kids."

Joey ran to his father. "No, Dad, don't go. You'll die."

Smith set his son away from him. "Joey, I'll die no matter what. I can die doing something good for a change or at the end of a rope on the gallows."

The tears Joey had so valiantly kept from shedding a little while ago now ran freely down his cheeks.

"You mind letting me ride your other horse over there?" Joe jutted his chin toward the stall with the second, big black horse.

"Not at all. Joey, why don't you saddle Beauty for your dad?"

Joey nodded. "Okay." He went over to the stall, picking up a horse blanket on his way.

Douglas looked over at the lad. "He's a good boy."

Smith followed his gaze. "Yes, he is. You take care of him and the rest of them, too."

Nodding, Douglas turned to Smith. "We will. I promise."

"Thank you. Go be with your wife. I'll help Joey saddle Beauty."

"Thanks."

She placed her hands on Douglas's chest and bunched his flannel shirt. "Is there nothing I can say to make you stay?"

He crushed her to him. "Nothing because you know this has to be."

"I know but I don't have to like it." She stood on her tiptoes and pressed a kiss to his lips. "Please be careful."

"I will."

Joe Smith walked over to them.

Joey followed behind his father leading both horses.

Douglas stepped away from Addie and mounted Star.

Smith mounted Beauty.

Looking down at the boy, Douglas said, "Joey, please hold the doors."

"Yes, sir." The boy walked both doors back open. They had closed a bit on their own.

Douglas gazed down at Addie. "I'll be back soon."

"You better be." She stepped back.

He touched his heels to Star's side.

The horse galloped out of the barn, followed by Smith on Beauty.

Addie watched him go, her heart with him, and prayed he'd be back. What would she do if he didn't?

CHAPTER THIRTEEN

Addie put her arm around Joey's shoulders and realized that in just a few months, he would be as tall as or taller than she was. He was growing so fast and yet, he was still just a boy who needed his father.

"They'll be all right."

He looked up at her, his eyes swimming with tears. "No, they won't. Dad said he would die…and he meant it. He don't want to swing at the end of a rope. I know what he done was wrong, but that was the whiskey. He was never that way before the whiskey got a hold of him." He wiped his eyes with the cuffs of his coat. "You saw him tonight. That's how he always used to be."

"I'm sorry as I can be, but your father has to pay

for what he did, whether it was because the whiskey had him or not. The whiskey didn't hit your mother, his fists did. He has to pay for that act. Do you understand, Joey?"

He nodded. "I do. I wish with all my heart that Mama was still alive." He pulled away from her hold. "I'll finish my chores. You can go on inside."

She followed him with her gaze as he walked to the cow and sat on the milk stool. His shoulders sagged under the weight of his feelings, but Addie also realized he needed to think everything through and come to his own decisions as to what he would do. Addie turned, left the barn and went back to the house.

Inside she found Claire straining the milk she'd gotten. "Will Joey be all right? I saw Father leave with Douglas and know how Joey must feel."

Addie put on her apron. "He'll be fine once he works it out in his mind and his heart. He's going through a difficult time. We should try to ease his burden."

The girl nodded. "I understand and will not mention Father in his presence."

"Thank you for gathering the eggs."

"You're welcome. When I saw you hadn't come out yet, I went ahead and gathered the eggs and brought them in with my milk."

Addie got out two large skillets, one for bacon and one for eggs. Once all two dozen eggs were clean, she made sure to leave six behind for cakes, cookies, whatever she decided to bake. She cracked the clean eggs into a bowl and scrambled them.

She finished the bacon and used a little of the grease in the egg pan. Preparing breakfast and caring for the children was something normal, something she could do to keep her mind and her hands busy so she didn't worry about Douglas and Joe.

Joey came in carrying another full milk pail.

"Put it on the counter please. I'll strain it in a minute and put it in the icebox."

Joey lifted the pail up to the counter. "I can do that." He got out the two-gallon milk can and cheesecloth. He poured the fresh milk through the cheesecloth into the can and put it in the icebox. Then he grabbed a pitcher and the milk can from yesterday out of the icebox. He poured the cold milk into the pitcher and placed it on the table.

Addie looked at her pin watch and saw that almost an hour had passed since the men left. She listened with her heart in her throat for the sound of horses returning. "Claire, set the table, please."

Joey grabbed plates from the cupboard. "I'll help." He looked over at Addie. "I need to keep busy."

She nodded and went back to stirring the eggs in the skillet. Frying the scrambled eggs didn't take long, and the children were beginning to file into the kitchen. Claire helped the youngest ones sit on a couple of books in a chair.

Addie turned to Claire. "Get Audrey, please but leave Emmy sleeping."

Just as Claire was leaving the kitchen, a loud bang sounded.

Addie did her best to remain calm. "Joey, you and Claire, get your brother and sisters into the living room and stay down. We don't know what caused that explosion."

Addie went outside, gun drawn, looked up toward the mine and saw a cloud of dust rising and knew the sticks Mack had set in the mine had exploded. Douglas said they would not go off, that they had been rendered safe. Apparently someone had reset the sticks to explode.

She placed her fist in her mouth to keep from screaming and scaring the kids. Nothing she could do but wait and go about her regular activities. But her eyes were swimming with tears and she had trouble seeing. Addie needed to go to Emmy and get her ready to eat.

In the babies' room, she found her youngest daughter awake and sucking her fist.

Addie cleaned her and changed her diaper and gown, putting her in a little dress. She picked her up and cuddled her. "How will you feel about a baby sister or brother? I bet you'll probably be jealous to begin with. You won't be the only baby by that time. Audrey will be walking and talking more than you will, but you'll catch up. Don't worry about that." She kissed Emmy's forehead. "Shall we go to the living room and get you fed? Yes? Then I think we shall."

In the kitchen, Claire had prepared a bottle for Emmy. "May I feed her?"

"Of course you may." She passed the baby to her new sister and heard horses outside at the same time. "Stay here." Addie ran out in time to see the rear of a horse entering the barn. Picking up her skirt, she ran. "Douglas!"

He turned and opened his arms.

She bounded into them. "I was so scared for you." Addie buried her face in his chest and sobbed.

"Shh. It's all right. Everything is fine." He tightened his hold on her. "It's okay, sweetheart."

Joey ran into the barn, his gaze searching. He closed his eyes tight. "He didn't make it out, did he?"

Douglas let Addie go and walked over to the boy. "No, someone had retriggered the dynamite in the mine after we had disconnected the sticks. He was rendering the new sticks safe when the last one exploded in his hand. The mine is buried under tons of rock and we'll be digging for days to reach him." He put his arm around Joey's shoulders. "He wanted it this way."

The boy nodded and then wrapped his arms around Douglas's waist holding him tight.

Her husband returned the embrace.

Addie clasped her hands in front of her, tears flowing freely down her cheeks.

Would life ever be the same?

Much later, Addie cuddled with her husband after making love, their union stronger than ever before. She felt closer to Douglas knowing that he loved her, too.

"I didn't want to ask earlier, but what about Cassidy? What happened to him? He didn't get away, did he?"

Douglas pulled her closer, if that was even possible. "I'm glad you didn't ask. I wouldn't have wanted to say anything in front of Joey. The dynamite did go off in Joe's hand that much was true. What I didn't say was, he came upon Robert placing that charge. They fought and Cassidy tried to run out of the mine. Joe set off the dynamite, burying him and Robert Cassidy under tons of rock. They were close enough I could see what was happening and far enough in to completely close the mine. Even if they survived the blast, which they couldn't, the gases and lack of air will kill them."

"I think Joey should know this. Know that his dad was a hero today, regardless of what he did in the past. I'm not saying he was a good man, because he wasn't. After all, he beat his wife to death and that can never be forgiven or understood or excused. But he did save his children in more ways than one. He signed the papers for the adoption, and he kept a bad man from taking you from them."

"I don't think so. What I told Joey is enough. He can make his own decision about the kind of man his father was. I think his opinion will change as he gets older and has a wife and children of his own. Then, and maybe not until then, will he realize what a heinous thing his father did."

"You're right. I was just trying to ease his grief, but I'm wrong. He needs to remember what his father did and that he needed to be punished for it. A life for a life. Saving one life doesn't make up for the one he took."

"That's right. I don't want to discuss this anymore. Just let me hold you and relish us being together and loving each other." He turned her in his arm so she was on her back. Then he put his hand on her belly. "We've created someone beautiful, boy or girl. Someone who is already loved and wanted more than I can express."

She smiled and covered his hand with hers. "We have. I will always be grateful that you married me, whatever your reasons."

"The only reason I had, was I couldn't let you go. I couldn't let another man have you. I fell in love with you but didn't know what it was, because I buried it under my anger at Elizabeth…and Josiah. I know now that she only went there to talk, otherwise he wouldn't have left all his worldly goods to you."

"I love you. I don't know what would have happened if I'd married Josiah, but I would have. My contract was with him, and I would have honored it."

"That's because you are a good, honorable woman. I know that now. I'll never doubt you again. Forgive me?"

She nodded, turned and kissed his chest.

He lifted her chin until she looked at him, then he covered her lips with his. When he pulled back, he ran his thumb over her bottom lip sensitive from his kisses. "I love you, Adeline Latimer. You hold my heart in your hands."

"And I love you. You're my husband and my heart."

He kissed her again and she felt all the love in his heart for her, for their children and for the child to come.

She finally felt whole. Her life suddenly made sense. All of her trials, being gambled by her father over and over again, were to bring her here. She wouldn't trade any of it for this moment. Addie hugged Douglas and rested her head on his chest. Content.

EPILOGUE

*S*eptember 23, 1872

*A*ddie lay in bed and breathed through the pain, waiting for the doctor to arrive. She'd been having light back pain since yesterday and bad pains all through the night and now morning was here and her baby was not. She was so tired.

Douglas held her hand with both of his and sat on the bed next to her.

"You don't have to stay." She said the words she was supposed to say though she didn't mean a one of them. "But I'm glad you're here."

He smiled down at her and then kissed her gently. "There is nowhere else I'd rather be. The younger kids are safe and happy with Joey and Claire to entertain them and the doctor is on his way."

"The doctor is here." Doc Collins barreled into the room and set his bag on the floor at the foot of the bed. "How are you feeling, Addie? I understand you're having contractions at regular intervals. How far apart are they now?"

"About three minutes. I waited until they were five minutes apart before I sent Joey for you."

"I'm sorry I was unavailable for the lad, but I was at another birth. Mrs. Raymond Gaines had a little boy to add to their five daughters. Ray was thrilled to finally have a son, but he never complained about only having girls." He went to the bureau and washed his hands in the basin there. "Who is helping you today? Or should I say helping me today?"

"Ester Partridge is here. She's downstairs getting some hot water. What she had earlier got cold while we waited."

Doc dried his hands on the provided towel. "Let's check and see how far along you are."

Douglas raised the sheet to Addie's waist for the doctor.

Addie spread her knees wide. "It feels like he's coming, but I've had that particular feeling for hours. Please tell me he's coming."

Ester came in carrying a bucket of water with a potholder around the handle.

"Ah, Ester, just in time," said Doc. "Will you open those curtains so I have light to see what we've got happening down here? It's liable to be dark soon and if the baby isn't here by then, we'll need a lamp."

She set down the bucket on the towel she'd brought up earlier and opened the curtains wide before coming to the side of the bed. "We be ready now, Doc."

He grinned.

Addie was sure it was for her benefit.

Doc returned his attention to her baby. "That's good. Now I see a bit of a crown so you need to push to get the little one out of the birth canal. So bear down and push with all your might." Doc watched her and then looked again at the baby.

After the exertion, Addie panted.

Doc gazed up at her through her knees. "All right, breathe now. Good, deep breaths. That's right. Now, I want you to push again. This time, harder than before, just as hard as you can. I know it will hurt, but you need to push through the pain. Do you understand?"

She nodded, too tired to speak.

"Okay, push. Push, Addie, push hard. Harder. Bear down."

"Douglas, help me lean up a little." He raised her body so she could lean up and push as hard as she could. She ignored the burning sensation and the stretching of her body…and pushed more. Then she felt the head pop out and stopped pushing. She caught her breath and fell back against the pillows.

Doc grinned again. "Now we need to get the rest of the baby out. You've got to grin and bear it. Push the baby out. You can do it. Come on now. Push. Push. Push. That's it, the baby is coming."

Addie felt the baby slide from her body.

Doc clipped and tied the umbilical cord.

Addie lifted herself onto her elbows, moaning as she did so.

Douglas supported her. "Is that better, sweetheart?"

Addie let out a long breath. "Yes, thank you."

"What do we have, Doc? Boy or girl?"

"This baby is a boy."

The doctor cleaned out the baby's mouth.

She heard the tiny cry emanating from her son.

"Ester, please take this baby and clean him up for his mama." Doc looked up at Addie. "Now we need to deliver the next baby."

Douglas, eyes wide, choked out, "Next baby?!"

Doc chuckled. "Yes, I wasn't sure until her last visit and by that late date, I figured I'd let you find out together. You need to push again, Addie. This one should be easier than the first. So just push as hard as you can."

Several pushing sessions later, the baby slid from her body.

Addie breathed heavily. "Well? What do we have this time?"

Doc smiled wide as he cleaned the baby's mouth "You have a second boy. Now you have to come up with names for both of them."

The baby started to cry.

"Here's another one for you Ester."

"We have one name picked out but hadn't even thought of a second," said Douglas, who was pale and whose eyes were still open wide.

Ester brought over the first baby and gave him to Addie. "Here you are, Addie, me lass."

Her brogue comforted Addie, for some reason. Ester was a good friend and their housekeeper. She was a wonderful cook and helped Addie with the cleaning and cooking. Claire helped, too, but seven children ages eleven down to thirteen months old proved too much for Addie and so Douglas hired Ester.

Soon she brought over the second baby and handed him to Douglas. "Now, Dougie, me lad, you get the smallest one. He's not very big but he has a fine set of lungs."

Addie laughed at Ester's nickname for Douglas.

He didn't seem to mind her calling him Dougie. Had anyone else tried it, they would have had words and not nice words either.

Addie's gaze rested on the baby in her arms and

then she opened his blanket to gaze at him. "He will be Douglas John Latimer, the second. He's the older of the two."

Douglas stared down at her and the baby. "I've been thinking about that. I don't want either of them to be or expect to be treated any differently than the other children. Their names should reflect that. I was thinking of Josiah and Joshua. Or Josiah and John. What are your ideas?"

She didn't raise her gaze from the baby. Addie touched his cheek and ran a hand over his dark hair. "I'm so glad you said something. I totally agree with you and that the first twin should be Josiah. But I think the second twin should be Frank. We don't have any children whose name begins with an *F*."

"Very well. What about their middle names?"

"Well, what was Josiah's middle name? Samuel, wasn't it?"

He nodded.

"Then it will be Josiah Samuel and Franklin John, after you."

Douglas grinned. "That works for me."

"I'll put those names in my book," said Doc. "I've finished my duties here. Ester can take care of the afterbirth in the bucket. I've placed thick cotton padding on you because you'll bleed." He placed his clean instruments back in his bag. "Ester can help you change it. I don't recommend trying to wash it. Just throw it away. If you run out of the padding, send someone for more from me. Now I'll take my leave. Those children of yours will want to come up and see the babies. They are in for as much a surprise as you two were."

Douglas nodded. "They can come up later, for now I want it to just be the four of us." He looked down at the baby Addie held and nodded toward him. "He does seem quite a lot bigger than this twin."

Doc shrugged. "I'm not worried about it. The little one will make up for it, I'm sure. If for some reason you're still worried in a month, I'll take a look and see if I can determine if anything is wrong."

"Thanks, Doc. What do I owe you?" asked Douglas.

"Five dollars will cover it, but you've got your hands full right now. I'll add it to your monthly bill."

Addie sighed. "How awful is that? We have a monthly bill at the doctor's."

"My dear girl," said Doc. "You have seven—no, nine children now. They will get hurt. They will break bones, get cuts and scrapes and knock out teeth. That's what kids do. I'd worry more if you didn't have a monthly bill for me. Then I'd wonder if you ever let your children have any fun."

Addie laughed and then winced, her muscles hurting from the strain they were under. "Oh, I think they have plenty of fun."

Doc nodded. "Just so. I'll see you in two weeks. Until then, if I don't hear from you, that's fine. Goodbye, now."

"Goodbye, Doc," said Addie, her gaze back on the baby in her arms.

The infant looked up at her as if to ask, "Are you my mama?"

"Bye, Doc," said Douglas.

Just as Doc was walking out, the children barreled in.

Doc raised his case over his head and made his way through the stampeding hoard.

"Let's see the baby," yelled Larry, who was just six and still seemed to have only one volume…loud.

"Where's our new baby?" asked Sara. She was five and very shy around strangers.

"Baba, baba, baba," said Audrey, who was twenty-two months.

Joey held Emmy who at thirteen months was walking…make that running…everywhere. She leaned over in Joey's arms to get him to let her down.

Claire carried Rami. She was four and rested her head on Claire's shoulder, her first two fingers in her mouth. "We're sorry but we heard Doc getting ready to leave and figured it was okay to come in now. Is it okay?"

Addie smiled and nodded. "Come closer and hold the little ones so they can see."

Douglas smiled at all the kids gathered around, as close as they could get to the bed. "Well, my children, you have two new brothers. Josiah and Frank."

Claire put down Rami and set her hands on her hips. "You had twins? Why didn't you tell us you were having twins? We could have prepared better. Now, all the little clothes we made will have to be shared and there won't be enough."

Laughing Addie put a free hand on Douglas's knee. "Because Doc Collins didn't tell us until the second one was being born."

Her eyes wide, Claire shook her head. "Is he crazy? I think that is something we should have known."

Nodding, Addie noticed Josiah was crying harder, though his little cries were so quiet, she could hardly hear him. After listening to Emmy and Audrey cry, his sounded more like squeaks. "I agree with you. This baby is hungry and I need to feed him. You all will get to see them again a little later."

Frank apparently heard his brother and he started crying, too.

"Ah, we don't wanna go," the littlest ones cried.

Claire took Rami and Sara by the hands and led them out of the room.

Joey picked up Emmy and Audrey and carried them.

Larry followed, but kept looking back and kicking at an invisible rock.

Ester came forward from over by the bureau. "I'll take this and dispose of it." She pointed toward a bucket. "Then I'll give them cookies and milk. That'll tide them over until dinner."

"Dinner? My gosh, what time is it?" asked Addie.

Ester looked at her pin watch. "It's about three-thirty in the afternoon."

Addie's mouth fell open. "My goodness, that took much longer than I expected. I've been in here for more than seven hours. Thank you, Ester. We appreciate you so much."

"That we do," agreed Douglas.

"Well, you and Dougie are my favorite people and now you've given me two new babies to spoil." Ester smiled, picked up the bucket and left the room.

Douglas closed, and locked the bedroom door after her.

Addie unwrapped Josiah and admired him.

Douglas did the same to Franklin. He took the babies and laid them side by side on the bed. "You can see how much smaller Franklin is. His poor little legs are just spindly."

"He'll be fine. I'll feed him first, so he gets plenty, although, for now it's going to be one breast per baby. But we can supplement with formula if we need to." She picked up Frank and placed him in her arm so she could hold him. She opened her nightgown and teased him with her nipple. After several failed attempts, the baby seemed to latch on and begin to nurse.

Addie winced and closed her eyes. "He seems to be feeding well. Will you place Josiah in my arm just like I have Frank?"

Douglas wrapped the baby back up and set him carefully in his mother's arm.

"You'll have to tease him with my nipple just like I did for Frank."

He did as she'd done and again, with trial and error, they managed to get both babies nursing. She did her best to not cry, but the nursing hurt. If she hadn't been told that nursing was best, despite the invention of powdered baby formula, she'd have stopped this process right away and only used bottles.

"Ah, sweetheart, don't cry. I'm so sorry it hurts."

"It's all right. Doc told me it would to begin with, but shortly it would be much better. It's just a matter of getting through these first few days."

Douglas lifted her chin until she looked into his eyes. "Have I told you lately, that I love you?"

She smiled. "I don't believe you have."

"I love you, Addie, with all my heart and soul."

"I love you, too, my heart, more than I ever thought possible. Thank you for my babies."

"You're welcome, my love."

Addie pursed her lips for a kiss.

Douglas didn't keep her waiting.

How did she get so lucky? To marry this man and have seven wonderful children, and then these two beautiful babies? Her father would have said that kind of luck only came along once in a lifetime.

And she would agree. She had her once in a lifetime love with her children and Douglas.

Nothing could get better than this.

ABOUT THE AUTHOR

Cynthia Woolf is an award-winning and best-selling author of forty-five historical western romance novels and six sci-fi romance novels, which she calls westerns in space. Along with these books she has also published four boxed sets of her books.

Cynthia loves writing and reading romance. Her first western romance Tame A Wild Heart was inspired by the story her mother told her of meeting Cynthia's father on a ranch in Creede, Colorado. Although Tame A Wild Heart takes place in Creede that is the only similarity between the stories. Her father was a cowboy not a bounty hunter and her mother was a nursemaid (called a nanny now) not the owner of the ranch.

Cynthia credits her wonderfully supportive husband Jim and her great critique partners for saving her sanity and allowing her to explore her creativity.

STAY CONNECTED!

Newsletter

Sign up for my newsletter and get a free book.

Follow Cindy

https://www.facebook.com/cindy.woolf.5
https://twitter.com/CynthiaWoolf
http://cynthiawoolf.com

ALSO BY CYNTHIA WOOLF

Bachelors and Babies

Carter

Brides of Homestead Canyon/Montana Sky Series

Thorpe's Mail-Order Bride

Kissed by a Stranger

A Family for Christmas

Bride of Nevada

Genevieve

Brides of the Oregon Trail

Hannah

Lydia

Bella

Eliza

Rebecca

Charlotte

Brides of San Francisco

Nellie

Annie

Cora

Sophia

Amelia

Brides of Seattle

Mail Order Mystery

Mail Order Mayhem

Mail Order Mix-Up

Mail Order Moonlight

Mail Order Melody

Brides of Tombstone

Mail Order Outlaw

Mail Order Doctor

Mail Order Baron

Central City Brides

The Dancing Bride

The Sapphire Bride

The Irish Bride

The Pretender Bride

Destiny in Deadwood

Jake

Liam

Zach

Hope's Crossing

The Stolen Bride

The Hunter Bride

The Replacement Bride

The Unexpected Bride

Matchmaker & Co Series

Capital Bride

Heiress Bride

Fiery Bride

Colorado Bride

The Surprise Brides

Gideon

Tame

Tame a Wild Heart

Tame a Wild Wind

Tame a Wild Bride

Tame A Honeymoon Heart

Tame Boxset

Centauri Series (SciFi Romance)

Centauri Dawn

Centauri Twilight

Centauri Midnight

Singles

Sweetwater Springs Christmas

Made in the USA
Las Vegas, NV
28 January 2021